A Note from Stephanie About the Bumpy Road to Fame

Did you ever have one of those days where *nothing* goes right? How about two days? A week? Well, I was having one and feeling like an absolute, total nobody. Definitely *un*-special. Then this big modeling contest was announced. And Amber Armstrong actually offered to share her secret fashion tips with me! Amber is only the most gorgeous girl in school and a professional model. With her on my side, I couldn't possibly lose. Unless, of course, Amber couldn't be trusted. . . .

But before I tell you more about my rise to fame, let me tell you about something really special. My family. My very *big* family.

Right now there are nine people and a dog living in our house—and for all I know, someone new could move in at any time. There's me, my big sister, D.J., my little sister, Michelle, and my dad, Danny. But that's just the beginning.

When my mom died, Dad needed help. So he asked his old college buddy, Joey Gladstone, and my Uncle Jesse to come live with us, to help take care of me and my sisters.

Back then, Uncle Jesse didn't know much about taking care of three little girls. He was more into rock 'n' roll. Joey didn't know anything about kids, either—but it sure was funny watching him learn!

Having Uncle Jesse and Joey around was like having three dads instead of one! But then something even better happened—Uncle Jesse fell in love. He married Rebecca Donaldson, Dad's co-host on his TV show, *Wake Up, San Francisco*. Aunt Becky's so nice—she's more like a big sister than an aunt.

Next Uncle Jesse and Aunt Becky had twin baby boys. Their names are Nicky and Alex, and they are adorable!

I love being part of a big family. Still, things can get pretty crazy when you live in such a full house!

FULL HOUSE™: Stephanie novels

Available from MINSTREL Books

FULL HOUSE™
Stephanie

Picture Me Famous

Lisa Simon

A Parachute Press Book

A MINSTREL® BOOK

Published by POCKET BOOKS
New York   London   Toronto   Sydney   Tokyo   Singapore

This book is a work of fiction. Names, characters, places and incidents are products of the author's imagination or are used fictiously. Any resemblance to actual events or locales or persons, living or dead, is entirely coincidental.

A MINSTREL PAPERBACK *Original*

A Minstrel Book published by
POCKET BOOKS, a division of Simon & Schuster Inc.
1230 Avenue of the Americas, New York, NY 10020

A PARACHUTE PRESS BOOK

READING   Copyright © 1995 by Warner Bros. Television

FULL HOUSE, characters, names and all related indicia are trademarks of Warner Bros. Television © 1995.

ISBN: 0-671-52276-0

First Minstrel Books printing October 1995

10 9 8 7 6 5 4 3

A MINSTREL BOOK and colophon are registered trademarks of Simon & Schuster Inc.

Cover photo by Schultz Photography

Printed in the U.S.A.

CHAPTER
1

◆ ◀ ◼ ◆

"Today's the day, Stephanie!" Allie Taylor cried.

"That's right." Darcy Powell held up her carrot stick like a microphone. "The day we've all been waiting for, ladies and gentlemen. And you'll see it happen right here, in the exciting John Muir Middle School cafeteria. An exciting thing happening in the cafeteria, you ask? Not possible, you say? Well, check it out, my friends. Today is the day that Stephanie Tanner will not only dream about, not only smile at, not only follow like a pathetic puppy, but will actually *speak* to the incredibly gorgeous—"

"And extremely popular," Allie added.

"—Kyle Sullivan!" Darcy finished in a hushed whisper.

Stephanie looked at her best friends and smiled weakly. "I'm not so sure about today, guys," she murmured. She tried to pretend that the food on her lunch tray was so appetizing that she couldn't take her eyes off it.

Stephanie peeked up through her bangs. Just as she suspected, neither Darcy nor Allie was going to let her change her mind. Darcy had her arms folded across her chest. Allie wore an I-mean-business look on her face.

"That's what you said yesterday!" Darcy complained. "There's no way we're going to let you chicken out—again!"

"Easy for you to say," Stephanie retorted. "You'll say anything to anybody." It was true, too. Darcy had once told the principal that the whole school should get her birthday off as a vacation day. Darcy was funny, popular, and outgoing. Looking like Whitney Houston's thirteen-year-old sister didn't hurt, either.

"What happened to the brand-new you?" Allie asked.

"Yeah!" Darcy nodded. "Remember your vow— no giggling or blushing when a boy came around. A boy, for example, by the name of Brandon Fallow?"

"Well," Stephanie said slowly, "I had two years

to get used to how gorgeous Brandon was. If he were still here, who knows?" Stephanie shrugged, trying to sound casual. "I might have already asked him on a date."

Darcy and Allie both burst out laughing.

"Yeah, right," Darcy sputtered. "Well, Steph, hate to burst your bubble, but Brandon's only gone to high school. You could find him if you really wanted to ask him out."

Stephanie's mind searched frantically for an excuse. "Maybe I should stay away from older men," she threw out. "My dad might not approve."

"Since when do you care if your dad approves of who you go out with?" Allie asked.

Stephanie had to admit she had no answer to that one. She decided to change the subject. "Kyle Sullivan, though, is still technically sort of new," Stephanie explained, twirling her fork through her mashed potatoes, "because of course he's my *new* crush—"

"Oh, right. Like you haven't spent every day of the last month thinking about nothing but Kyle, Kyle, Kyle," Darcy said with a smirk.

"I *have* been studying for tests and writing tons of papers, you know," Stephanie replied. Truth was, she was totally stumped about what her next English paper would be about.

"More like studying Kyle's every move and writing imaginary love letters to him," Allie said, brushing her wavy brown hair from her face.

They're not buying it. Stephanie sighed to herself.

"Didn't we discuss Kyle strategy all weekend?" Allie continued. "We decided that you would make the first move and ask him to go to the football game Friday night."

Stephanie glanced nervously across the lunchroom. Kyle Sullivan was at his usual table with the rest of the ninth-grade boys. He looked as gorgeous as ever in a white turtleneck and black jeans. If there was anyone who could take Brandon's place in her heart, this was the boy!

Stephanie knew every detail of his face. Which wasn't a great surprise, she supposed, considering she'd spent so much time staring at it. His hair was golden blond and wavy. His nose was nice and straight, with a few freckles across it. And his brown eyes had little flecks of gold in them. On top of all that perfection, his right front tooth was a *tiny* bit chipped at the corner. It was Stephanie's favorite thing about him.

Lately she'd been thinking about him more and more, and last night she'd even dreamt about him. It was definitely starting to interfere with her schoolwork. Not to mention her breathing.

4

"Okay." Stephanie sighed again. "If I don't do something soon, I might lose it completely."

"You'd better hurry," Darcy warned, "or someone else is going to beat you to him. In fact"—she shook her head—"you may have just missed your chance."

"Oh, no!" Allie whispered. "It's Rene Salter!"

Stephanie almost couldn't bring herself to watch. Rene was one of the senior Flamingoes. The Flamingoes were an exclusive club of snobby girls who thought they were the most popular kids in school. They wore pink clothes all the time, and they'd only invite you to be a Flamingo if they thought you were cool enough for them. Stephanie and Darcy had been asked to join the club when they were just sixth graders, and they almost had. Until Stephanie found out that the Flamingoes were just using her for her father's phone card. Ever since then, things between Stephanie and the Flamingoes hadn't been exactly friendly.

Stephanie watched as Rene approached Kyle. She couldn't hear the conversation, but she did see Kyle shrug. Rene leaned down and spoke again, and then Kyle shook his head no. The other boys at the table chuckled as Rene stalked away, her face turning red.

"Looks like she struck out," Darcy said, smiling.

"And that's supposed to make *me* feel better?" Stephanie asked. "She's only one of the most popular girls in school." Even after an entire weekend of planning, Stephanie still didn't know if she was ready to talk to Kyle.

"Well, he doesn't like Rene and neither do we," Allie pointed out. "That's a good start. Something you two will have in common."

"He's done eating," Darcy said. "You've got to talk to him now!"

"Yeah, he's about to take his tray back." Allie nodded.

"I can't!" Stephanie said, her heart beating faster. "I have to—"

"You have to what?" Darcy and Allie said at the same time.

Stephanie looked desperately down at her tray. "I have to . . . finish my beets." She speared the slice of purple vegetable with her fork and looked up at Darcy and Allie. Neither girl cracked even the teeniest smile.

"Okay, okay," Stephanie said, rising shakily.

"He dropped a spoon," Allie said.

"Now he's heading for the garbage," Darcy whispered.

"Be quiet, already," Stephanie said through

6

clenched teeth. "This isn't the Olympics. We don't need a play-by-play."

"Well, then, get moving!" Darcy urged.

Stephanie turned toward the garbage cans. *Take a deep breath*, she told herself. *And relax. You just have to say ten little words. You've practiced them over and over.*

Even though Stephanie had carried a lunch tray across the cafeteria practically every day of her life, she suddenly felt nervous and awkward, as though she were about to spill everything or trip over her own feet. She tried to walk normally, but her knees were knocking. And her throat felt like it was glued shut with peanut butter. This was terrible! How would she say anything to him if she couldn't talk?

Ten little words.

Kyle, are you going to the football game Friday night?

As Stephanie stepped forward, everything seemed to be happening in slow motion. Kyle approached the garbage can. He brushed his hair out of his eyes with his left hand. He tilted his tray. Stephanie watched his apple core slide into the garbage. Then he bent over and slid his tray onto the top of a nearby pile.

Kyle, are you going to the football game Friday night?

In one second, he'd be gone.

Stephanie took a breath, smiled, and said loudly, "Football, are you going to the Kyle game Friday night?"

Her hand flew to her mouth.

Stephanie closed her eyes. Her head spun dizzily and she felt like fainting. She wished that the ground would open up and swallow her. She wanted to disappear off the face of the earth. Forever!

Ten little words, and she had completely blown them.

"Would you like to go to the football game Friday night?" Kyle said.

Stephanie's eyes popped open and her jaw dropped. *Can this really be happening?* she thought. *Unbelievable! Kyle is asking me out anyway! Even though I just called him a football!* Stephanie looked up and saw his handsome face, those gorgeous brown eyes looking right at her.

"Would you excuse me?" he muttered as he moved by her, his eyes shifting to something behind her.

Stephanie turned her head in disbelief. Kyle hadn't been speaking to her at all! He'd been talking to someone else the whole time. Someone standing right behind her.

Someone in a black bodysuit, a big leather belt,

jeans, and tan suede cowboy boots. Someone who looked like she should be on the cover of a magazine instead of in the middle school cafeteria.

Stephanie swallowed hard.

It was the new girl, Amber Armstrong.

"Friday night?" Amber said vaguely, looking away from Kyle.

"Oh, come on," Kyle pressed. "It'll be fun."

Stephanie had noticed Amber the first day she'd arrived. Who hadn't? Amber was beautiful—tall and slim with a perfect face, deep blue eyes, and long, strawberry blond hair.

"Well, I'm afraid I'm busy that night," Amber answered, tossing her hair over her shoulder. "Sorry."

Suddenly Stephanie realized she'd been standing there, slack jawed, staring at Kyle and Amber. Convinced that she would explode if she didn't get out of the cafeteria in two seconds, she dumped everything into the garbage can, tray included, and ran for the doors. She brushed past Darcy and Allie without saying a word. They didn't let her go far, though. Darcy grabbed her arm before she took off down the hall. "What happened, Steph?"

"I'm so embarrassed!" Stephanie cried, looking over her shoulder to see if anyone else was coming out of the cafeteria. She leaned against the wall and let her head fall back with a thunk against the hard cinder blocks.

"I'm such an idiot." She sighed.

"Tell us what happened," Allie urged.

"I completely messed up my line." Stephanie groaned. "His name is Kyle and I called him a football!" she wailed.

"Huh?" Darcy said. "Run that by me again."

Allie looked dumbfounded and shook her head.

"Oh, never mind. Just believe me when I tell you I blew it, big time. I totally botched it, but that doesn't matter anyway, because he asked Amber Armstrong to go to the game!"

"Really?" Allie said. "And what did she say?"

"She said no," Stephanie replied. "Can you believe it?"

"That's good, Steph. It means you have nothing to worry about," Darcy said.

"But he must have a big crush on her," Stephanie pointed out.

"He's probably just trying to be nice," Allie said. "You know, because she's new and all."

"Right. And you're going to tell me it makes no difference that she's totally gorgeous?" Stephanie made a face.

"Maybe," Allie admitted. "But she's really shy.

10

She's in my math class and she never says a word. I don't think she has any friends yet."

"Maybe not any *girl* friends," Stephanie said sadly.

"Stephanie, he just asked her out for one date," Darcy assured her. "They may not even like each other."

"Yeah," Stephanie agreed halfheartedly. "There's no reason why two of the most perfect-looking people on planet Earth would like each other. I mean, it's not like they have anything in common."

"If you had talked to him yesterday—" Darcy began.

Stephanie rolled her eyes. "Thanks for cheering me up, Darce." Just then the bell rang. Stephanie tried to pull herself together, flicking her bangs and tucking in her shirt.

"By the end of the day, you'll forget all about it," Allie said, giving Stephanie a thumbs-up sign.

"I hope so," Stephanie agreed, waving good-bye. "Or you'll both be the ones to suffer."

"Hey! Why's that?" Allie asked.

"Because it was your idea to talk to him," Stephanie said.

"Because you had no room in your brain for

11

any other idea," Darcy teased, "once *Kyle* moved in there."

"I guess this definitely means I have to move him out," Stephanie murmured to herself. Easier said than done.

Stephanie sat through her history class in a daze. She couldn't stop thinking about what had happened in the cafeteria. She kept picturing the scene over and over, where she blew her line and Kyle stepped past her to get to Amber.

"And we hope to see you tomorrow, *Stephanie*," Ms. Shapot called out. Stephanie looked up, startled, and realized the room was completely empty. She hadn't even heard the bell ring for the end of class. Picking up her notebook, she shuffled out with a sheepish smile for Mrs. Shapot.

She was thankful English was next. Maybe Ms. Simms could take her mind off the cafeteria disaster. Stephanie might not be great with words when it came to talking to handsome older boys named Kyle, but she was good with words when it came to writing.

She felt a twinge of guilt as she watched Ms. Simms passing back their homework. Stephanie knew she hadn't put much work into her essay. How could she have? She'd spent all weekend with Darcy and Allie, talking about Kyle.

So if I don't get an A this time, it won't kill my average, Stephanie thought. *I'll just do better next time.*

"I can't believe it!" Alyssa Norman cried, turning over the paper Ms. Simms had put on her desk. "I got a C-minus!"

Stephanie fought to hide her grin. It was hard not to gloat just a little when one of the Flamingoes got what she deserved. Alyssa was known throughout school for cheating on tests and copying other kids' homework.

Alyssa turned to the girl behind her. "I thought you said that writing about endangered species would get me an A for sure! Well, you can just forget being in the Flamingoes now!"

"I said whales or dolphins," the other girl whined. "Not your brother's dead goldfish."

Stephanie shook her head. That was pretty typical for a Flamingo. The truth was that a *good* writer could make a story about anything—even goldfish—into a *good* story. The problem was that writing was hard, and not everyone had the talent for it.

Stephanie smiled in anticipation as she flipped her own paper over.

Then she almost had a heart attack.

She couldn't believe what she saw at the top

of the paper, written in big letters in dark red marker.

C-plus!

Stephanie was in shock. She knew the story wasn't her best. And she knew she hadn't spent much time on it. But a C-plus! There had to be some mistake! She did almost as bad as one of the Flamingoes.

English was her best subject—wasn't it?

Stephanie kept blinking at the huge red C-plus, hoping it would disappear or turn into something else. This was the worst grade she had ever gotten in her entire life!

"Now remember, class," Ms. Simms said. "You have a big research paper due, and I want topics from you in two weeks." She looked around the room, and then her gaze rested on Stephanie. "I think some of you should use this time wisely."

Stephanie looked down quickly and saw that Ms. Simms had written a note in the margin, right next to a little frowning face. As Stephanie read it, she frowned herself.

We both know you can do a lot better than this, Stephanie. Spend more time on your work and stick to writing about what you know.

"I thought I knew how to write," Stephanie muttered sadly. Hadn't all her other English teachers

14

always said she was a great writer? Could they all have been lying?

What a day she was having. First she couldn't get the words out of her mouth. Now it seemed she couldn't get them down on paper, either.

Can't I do anything right? Stephanie said to herself.

CHAPTER
2

◆ ◀ ◖ ◆

"Why are you so bummed?" Darcy asked as Stephanie met her friends by the pay phone after class. "You look worse than you did after lunch! And I didn't think that was possible."

"Thanks a lot, Darce," Stephanie said, giving her a dirty look. "I just got back a paper in English," she went on, "and I got a C-plus."

Allie stared. "But you're the total best at English," she cried. "I don't understand. What happened?"

"What else? I spent all weekend with you guys talking about Kyle instead of researching my story," Stephanie said.

"Oh, boy," Darcy muttered. "This is one of those Danny-Tanner-lecture-for-sure situations, isn't it?"

"Don't remind me." Stephanie moaned. "You know him—always saying how I'm going to be a famous writer someday."

"It's only one bad grade," Allie said hopefully.

"I can hear your dad now," Darcy said. " 'One bad grade is one too many.' "

"Darcy, is this supposed to make me feel better?" Stephanie asked.

"Ooops, sorry," Darcy said.

"Well, good luck," Allie said.

Darcy squeezed Stephanie's arm. "Call me tonight if you get grounded."

"Grounded?" Stephanie shouted after her. "Give me a break!" Sometimes Darcy had a way of saying the very worst thing when she was trying to cheer you up.

Stephanie felt a little guilty as she watched her friends walk away. She hadn't told them the whole truth about the English grade. It wasn't only her father who'd be disappointed. Stephanie herself had often dreamed about becoming a famous writer. She often pictured herself walking into a bookstore and seeing her name in big letters on the cover of a best-selling novel.

But a C-plus made it kind of hard to keep imagining that. *Maybe I'm not really cut out to be a writer after all*, Stephanie said to herself as she made her way to her locker. *I mean, professional writers have to write really well every day. They have to write A-plus material every time, not C-plus.*

Well, if I'm not a talented writer, maybe it's time I find something else to be talented at, Stephanie decided.

Something that I'm really good at. Something that will make me famous.

Something that will make Kyle notice me.

The same way he noticed Amber Armstrong.

When Stephanie opened the front door of her house, Alex and Nicky, her four-year-old cousins, ambushed her on her way to the kitchen. They each grabbed one of her hands and said, "Look, Stephanie. A doghouse."

"What? The doghouse is in—" Then Stephanie saw what the boys were pointing to. In the middle of the living-room floor sat Comet, with the couch cushions and pillows banked up on all sides of him. The twins had made a doghouse for their golden retriever with the pillows, draping an afghan over the entire structure. Comet looked nice and cozy in his new home, Stephanie decided.

Just then her uncle Jesse came running from the kitchen, fresh tomato sauce stains on his apron and his shiny black hair almost standing on end.

"Uncle Jesse," Stephanie asked, "what are you doing home? I thought you'd be practicing for your gig."

"Well, I should be." Jesse sighed. "I'm trying to write a new song right now." He pointed to his electric guitar, propped up on a chair. "Except that I have to make dinner and watch these little guys. Becky had to interview someone for the show. Your dad's still at work, too."

Stephanie nodded. Her aunt Becky and her dad were coanchors of the television show *Wake Up, San Francisco*. Jesse, Becky, and the twins lived in an apartment in the attic.

Jesse was a rock musician, and Stephanie loved to hear him play with his band. He even wrote and sang his own songs. *Gee*, Stephanie thought, *I come from a family of talented entertainers. Maybe some of that talent will rub off on me.*

"Hey, watch out!" Jesse cried, lunging for his guitar as Comet walked into the chair the guitar was propped on. Apparently Comet had grown tired of being inside the doghouse and needed to stretch a bit. But his sight was obstructed by the afghan that had been serving as the roof of the doghouse, and he couldn't see where he was going. Alex and Nicky giggled and pulled off the afghan.

"Steph!" Jesse said brightly, suddenly snapping his fingers. "I know we didn't ask you to baby-sit tonight, but since you're here . . . and I'm going crazy—"

"Let me guess," Stephanie teased, putting her finger to her forehead, "you want some help with the boys?"

Jesse smiled weakly. Stephanie wondered why, with all the people living in her house, she was always the one who got asked to baby-sit.

Stephanie looked at Jesse and had to laugh. He was giving her his "please, please, please" grin. It was the same one that the twins used—impossible to turn down.

"Okay, okay," Stephanie agreed, laughing. "I'll do it, but only if you play your new song for me."

"Deal." Jesse picked up his electric guitar and threw the strap over his shoulder.

"Come here, guys," Stephanie said to the twins.

Jesse put one knee up on a chair and leaned over the guitar. He started plucking slowly. Loud music came from the small amplifier set up next to the table.

"You can sing along to this one," Jesse said.

"Me?" Stephanie asked, surprised. "I can't sing."

"Even a person without a great voice can sing the blues. You just have to kind of talk it through.

20

The melody is easy. Besides," he added, "you've got a nice voice."

A nice voice? Stephanie thought. *That's news to me!* "Thanks, Uncle Jesse," she said.

Jesse strummed a few chords. "I'm trying to re-work an oldie. You know, make it a little more hip. Try it."

"Okay," Stephanie agreed.

"I ain't got . . . that hurtin' feeling . . . Seeing you . . . don't send me reeling . . . 'cause it's done, done, done, whoa oh oh oh," Jesse sang.

Stephanie hummed along with him for a few more bars, until a timer went off in the kitchen.

"Oops," Jesse said, setting the guitar back down. "Gotta get back to the food. So, what do you think?"

"Uh—the song's great," Stephanie said, her mind suddenly whirling. *It was right in front of me all along,* she thought. A new talent! "Do you really think I've got a nice voice?"

"Sure," Jesse replied. "Why?"

"Oh, no reason," Stephanie said, getting excited. "Uncle Jesse, will you show me a few guitar chords?"

"Sure," Jesse answered, heading back to the kitchen. "There's the guitar. Play around with it a little. I'll give you a lesson later if you just keep your eyes on the boys."

21

Stephanie picked up the guitar and flung the strap over her shoulder the way she'd seen Jesse do, but it fell right off. She was too short for it. So she put her foot up on the chair and balanced the guitar on her leg.

This is a great *way to be famous*, Stephanie thought, her eyes shining while she imagined it. She could have her own all-girl band, the San Francisco Stompers.

Stephanie strummed the guitar strings once. A loud twangy noise came from the amplifier. It didn't sound much like a chord, but Stephanie figured she could learn those later. She started strumming slowly.

"Kyle . . . Kyle . . . you didn't call me . . . you didn't dial . . . the telephone!" Stephanie sang loudly.

Alex and Nicky put their hands over their ears.

"This is the blues, guys," Stephanie called to them. "You're too young to appreciate it."

"Bar—neee!" the boys cried.

"No, no," Stephanie said. "Barney doesn't get the blues." She started strumming again, this time with a little more rhythm. *"Kyle . . . Kyle . . . you trashed me at the trash can . . . all for that Amber . . . maybe I'll . . ."* Stephanie paused, her fingers still strumming the strings while she thought.

22

"Maybe I'll ram her!" Stephanie cried. *"Even if she is new . . . she doesn't deserve you!*

"Oh, Ms. Simms," Stephanie moaned, *"what's all the fuss . . . How could you do it . . . give me that nasty C-plus!"*

Suddenly Comet started barking loudly. Stephanie's little sister, Michelle, came racing into the room with her fingers in her ears.

"Oh, it's you!" Michelle cried, her eyes wide. "I thought I heard a fire alarm."

The front door opened and D.J., Stephanie's older sister, came into the living room, tossing her jean jacket onto the couch. Stephanie continued to play, only dimly hearing her sister say something to her.

"Jeez, is that you, Steph?" D.J. asked. "I could hear the noise from down the block. All the dogs in the neighborhood are barking and whining. Are you planning to write a story about how you drove the dogs in town crazy?"

Stephanie kept up her jam session of one. She was really getting into it.

At that moment Jesse came back out of the kitchen.

"How's it going, Stephanie?" he asked. "I couldn't quite hear your singing because the dog in the yard next door was barking so loudly."

"Hey, everyone," Danny said, taking off his jacket and hanging it on the hook by the door.

"Did you get dinner finished, honey?" Becky called to Jesse, bending down to hug the twins as they ran at her.

Just then the phone rang. "Someone get that," Danny yelled on top of Comet's barking and the ringing phone. Stephanie stopped playing to see if it was either Darcy or Allie calling her.

Michelle answered it, with one finger still in an ear.

"Hold on," she said, walking over to Stephanie and holding out the portable phone to her. "It's for you."

Stephanie took the phone and put it to her ear. "Hello?"

"Hello, this is Mrs. Dominick, your neighbor."

"Yes," Stephanie said. "Can I help you?"

"Look, I'm sorry to bother you, but could you turn down the volume on your radio? And maybe you could change the station while you're at it. We usually like music, too—but the dog is howling and my husband is getting a headache."

"Of course." Stephanie sighed. "No problem."

"Thanks, dear. I appreciate it. It's really driving Daisy *crazy*."

Stephanie clicked the button and hung up. She

looked around the room. No one seemed to appreciate how hard she was struggling to develop her musical talent. Comet had tried to crawl under the couch. Alex, Nicky, and Michelle had climbed under the doghouse pillows. Becky and Danny had pained expressions on their faces. D.J. was looking for her Walkman to block out the sound.

"Listen, guys," Stephanie began.

"We're trying not to," D.J. said.

"You just don't understand. An up-and-coming musical sensation has to start somewhere."

"Yeah, like the bottom," D.J. said.

"D.J., go set the table," Danny ordered.

"Look, dinner's ready anyway," Jesse said, taking the guitar from Stephanie. "We'll practice afterward, okay, Steph?" Jesse bent down and flicked the amplifier knob. "And maybe next time, we'll keep this off," he added.

As Stephanie started walking into the kitchen, Joey entered through the front door. "Gee, I don't know what's going on out there. The dogs are all howling like monsters, and it's not even a full moon."

"Time for dinner," Jesse said. "You just missed the Stephanie Tanner show."

"So, Stephanie," Danny said after they'd all settled in at the dinner table. "I didn't know Jesse was teaching you to play the guitar." He looked over at her. "That's a terrific idea. A talent for music runs in the family."

"And stops with Stephanie," D.J. quipped.

"Thanks a lot." Stephanie frowned.

"Maybe you'll be famous!" Michelle cried.

"Famous for driving everyone out of town!" D.J. cracked.

Everyone laughed—except Stephanie.

"Are you writing your own songs again, Steph?" Danny asked, trying to be helpful. Everyone in the family remembered how Stephanie had recently gotten herself into a jam. She'd promised to get a famous rock group to write a song for her school project. In the end she'd had to write it herself! At least she'd written the words to the song. Jesse had written the music. But the song was a huge hit at school.

"She's not writing this time," Jesse answered for her. "This time she's singing. Singing the blues."

"Yeah, she sings and we all get blue!" Joey joked. Joey Gladstone, Danny's old college roommate who now lived with the family, was a professional comedian. But sometimes—like right now—Stephanie didn't think he was all that funny.

"*Do* you have something to be sad about, Stephanie?" Becky asked with concern, looking at her closely.

"Besides your singing," D.J. added.

"May I be excused, Dad?" Stephanie asked, putting down her fork. "I'm not that hungry, and I have some important homework to do."

"Sure," Danny said. "As long as nothing's wrong."

Stephanie shook her head. The only thing wrong was how everything she tried was always a joke to the rest of her family. And then there was her really bad grade. And the fact that she had no topic for her next paper. Plus the sad truth that Kyle liked someone else. And the fact that she had absolutely no special talent at all! Other than that, everything was just peachy!

"So how's the homework?" Danny asked later, poking his head into Stephanie's bedroom. "You seemed pretty anxious to get to it."

"It's okay, I guess." Stephanie looked down at the notebook she'd been doodling in for the last hour. She'd been trying to come up with a topic for her paper, but so far all she'd come up with was fifty different ways to write Kyle's name.

"I thought Jesse was going to give you a music lesson after dinner. Did something happen?" Danny asked.

"By order of Joey, my sisters, the neighborhood, and the Dog Lovers Association of America," Stephanie replied glumly, "I'm not having a lesson."

"Well, don't get too upset," Danny said. "It takes time to develop a talent."

"I know." Stephanie sighed. "And that's only part of the problem." She hesitated, then pulled her English paper off her desk. Might as well get it over with. "I have something to show you," she said to her dad, and held out the paper to him.

"Well," Danny said slowly, "this is a surprise."

"I know." Stephanie dropped her chin into her hands. "I'm sorry."

"I hope so," Danny replied, handing Stephanie back her paper. "And I hope you'll take Ms. Simms's advice." He smiled at her kindly and stood up.

"You're not going to give me a lecture?" Stephanie's eyes opened wide with shock.

"I think you've realized your mistake. And if you've learned from it, there's no need for a lecture."

"Wow! You mean it, Dad?" Stephanie said, amazed. *Wait till I tell Darcy and Allie how easy he let me off,* she thought.

"Look, if you really want that lecture I can still give it to you," Danny said, and then began.

"When I was your age and I got anything less than an A-plus, my father told me I couldn't watch TV for a whole month!"

"Oh, Dad. I know you're lying. They didn't have TV back then!" Stephanie joked.

Danny looked shocked and offended. Then he said, "But seriously, Steph. I trust you. That's why you're missing out on my lecture—this time."

Danny put his arm around her shoulders. "And honey, I know how awful you feel. I heard you downstairs trying to drown your sorrows in that song."

"But you came home after I stopped singing," Stephanie said in confusion.

"Well," Danny admitted, "actually we got home before that, and we heard the racket . . . I mean, we heard you practicing, and we thought we'd just wait outside for a few minutes—"

"I get it." Stephanie groaned, leaning her head on his shoulder. "Don't try to make me feel better. My singing was worse than my English grade!"

"That's not what really matters, though," Danny said.

"I know," Stephanie replied. "I promise I'll work harder on my paper next time."

Danny smiled. "I'm sure you will."

When Danny left, Stephanie kicked off her shoes

and flopped down on her bed. *I have to find another way to feel special again,* she thought. A new talent. *It isn't going to be writing, and according to the dog population of San Francisco, it isn't going to be singing, either!*

So what's it going to be?

CHAPTER
3

The next morning, after their media lab class, Stephanie and Allie met Darcy by the pay phone and Stephanie recapped the night's events.

"Poor Comet," Allie teased. "You know how high-pitched noises really hurt a dog's ears."

"Please don't start a dog frenzy on my block," Darcy begged. "My neighbors have those big kinds of dogs—the kind that can pull your car out of a ditch or something."

"Well," Stephanie said, feeling better about the whole night now that her friends had made her laugh, "I'm pretty sure singing is out."

"Does that mean we can't be in your band?" Allie asked.

"Lucky for you." Stephanie smiled. "See you at lunch."

Later Stephanie sat on one of the locker-room benches, lazily tugging on her gym socks and sneakers. Gym was definitely her least-favorite class. Stephanie was always looking for excuses to get out of it, and she really wished she had one for today. The last thing she needed was to have her gym teacher blowing her whistle and yelling at her for not running fast enough or doing the right kind of push-ups.

Stephanie liked to dance more than she liked to play sports. There was a time when she liked to watch team sports—especially football. But now, after what had happened in the cafeteria yesterday, she never wanted to see another football game as long as she lived.

Stephanie grimaced as she remembered what she'd said: *"Football, are you going to the Kyle game Friday night?"*

She rose from her bench and headed for the gymnasium. There was no use putting off the inevitable. Even if she didn't enjoy gym, at least she loved her new sneakers. They were white cross-trainers with bright blue soles. And she had on her oversize shorts with the purple stripes down the sides. Just because she didn't like gym didn't mean she had to look bad while doing it.

As Stephanie pushed open the locker-room door she wondered what kind of physical torture she was in for today. She was surprised to see the girls' gym packed with both girls and boys. It looked like half the school was there! *What are they all doing in here?* Stephanie wondered. *Fourth period starts in five minutes.*

Everyone was crowded around the gymnastics equipment. Stephanie stood on tiptoe and tried to peer over all the heads in front of her.

"Wow," she heard a girl from her gym class mutter, "she's incredible! How does she do that to her body?"

Stephanie saw Darcy and Allie on the other side of the crowd. Allie waved and shook her head, raising her eyebrows as though she were saying, "Isn't it amazing?"

Stephanie saw her gym teacher, Ms. Nugent, gaping at something or someone. Her whistle dangled from her hand and there was a look of total admiration on her face.

Suddenly everyone stepped back. Stephanie caught a glimpse of long golden hair flying through the air as someone leapt from the floor mat up onto the balance beam.

Stephanie shook her head and blinked to make sure she wasn't imagining things. But the image remained.

It was Amber Armstrong.

Amber Armstrong poised delicately on the balance beam, her toes pointed, her arms held gracefully above her head. Amber was wearing an orange leotard that hugged her perfect figure and accented the color of her long hair.

Suddenly Amber bent backward and kicked up her legs, balancing in a handstand. Her arms shook just slightly as she held the difficult position.

Stephanie could feel everyone around her holding their breath until Amber came down again. Still perfectly balanced, she slid right into a full split.

"How does she do that?" Stephanie heard a boy whisper. "That beam is only about four inches wide!"

"I don't know how she does it," his friend replied. "But she's *excellent.*"

Stephanie recognized both voices. She turned around.

And looked directly at Kyle. He looked back at her and smiled and nodded casually. Stephanie had lost faith in her language skills where Kyle was concerned, so she just smiled and nodded, too. Kyle was talking to Ian Ezratty, Stephanie's long-time friend and star of the basketball team. Two of the coolest boys in school, talking about Amber Armstrong.

Stephanie turned her head just in time to watch Amber take three small steps and launch into a no-handed flip. She landed on the beam perfectly, with only a small puff of chalk rising from her feet. Around her the crowd burst into applause.

Stephanie realized she was clapping along. She couldn't help herself. It was like watching the Olympics. Amber Armstrong *was* excellent. And incredible. And amazing.

And Stephanie couldn't help feeling a twinge of jealousy. As she watched Amber's beaming smile and her flushed face, she began imagining how nice it would feel to be so good at something. Stephanie sighed wistfully and turned away.

Looking good was fine, Stephanie thought, checking out her own gym outfit. But *being* good was what really mattered.

And Amber Armstrong was both.

"Hey, Steph!" Allie cried running over. "Did you see that?"

"Wasn't she great?" Darcy exclaimed. "She should be a professional or something. Awesome!"

"Yeah," Stephanie agreed halfheartedly. "She's great."

Darcy cocked her head and looked at Stephanie strangely. "You did see the same thing we saw, didn't you?" she asked.

"How could I miss it?" Stephanie replied. "There was practically a stampede to get close to her."

The crowd thinned as students began hurrying to their classes. Everyone was going to be late, but nobody seemed to mind. *I guess they think she was worth it*, Stephanie decided.

Meanwhile Amber stood wiping chalk dust from her hands. Then she stepped off the mat, grabbed her bag, and began walking toward Stephanie to get back to the locker rooms.

"Hey, Amber," Allie cried. "You were great!"

Amber seemed startled as she paused. "Oh, thanks."

"Too bad you're not in my gym class," Allie continued. "Because if you were, you could practice for us every day. All we'd have to do is watch you, and I doubt Ms. Nugent would mind one bit!"

"Yeah," Amber said quickly, looking away. "Well, thanks. But I . . . uh, I changed my schedule so that I could practice through lunch if I wanted."

"Wow!" Allie said. "You must really like gymnastics if you'd miss lunch to practice."

"You were fantastic!" Darcy added. "You should get a gold medal for that."

"Thanks," Amber replied.

Stephanie noticed that Amber was slowly inching backward.

"Are you going to practice through lunch today?" Allie asked. "If you're not, you could eat with us."

Stephanie looked up quickly. *I don't remember Allie being this outgoing or friendly with anyone else before,* she thought. *She must really like Amber.*

"Oh. Well . . ." Amber chewed her lip, keeping her eyes down. "Actually, no. Not today. I have to do something else during lunch today."

Stephanie tried to push off another pang of jealousy. Allie knew that Kyle had asked Amber to the football game yesterday. Surely she could understand that Stephanie would have a hard time eating lunch with Amber.

"Thanks for asking," Amber said. "I'm sorry, I've got to go now." Amber turned and practically bolted back to the locker room.

"You did say gold medal, didn't you?" Stephanie said to Darcy. "Like in the Olympics?"

"Why? What do you mean?" Darcy asked.

"It's just that Olympic athletes are supposed to be really friendly." Stephanie shrugged. "You know, ambassadors to the world and all that."

"She's probably just embarrassed," Allie said.

"What?" Stephanie cracked. "Embarrassed to be seen with us?"

"Embarrassed 'cause of all the attention she got," Allie said. "What's wrong with you, Stephanie?"

"Nothing. I just think she's not being very friendly, that's all. And I bet she's used to all the attention."

"She should be," Darcy said. "She's really talented."

And pretty. And the girl that Kyle's got his eye on, Stephanie thought, glancing at the empty balance beam. *So what does that make me?*

"We'd better get to class," Allie said, checking her watch. "We're really late."

"Hey, Steph, cheer up," Darcy called as they hurried away. "You're lucky to have Amber in your gym class now—maybe you won't even have gym today." She giggled. "I think Ms. Nugent's seen too many flips already."

CHAPTER
4

◆ ◢ ◣ ◆

It took Stephanie so long to change back into her school clothes after gym class that she was late for lunch. And she got stuck at the end of the lunch line, after all the decent food had already been picked over. Slowly she made her way to the table she shared with Darcy and Allie. She set down her tray and carefully lowered herself onto a chair. She couldn't help wincing as she sat.

"What happened? Are you okay?" Darcy asked, looking at her worriedly.

"What was the last thing you said to me?" Stephanie reminded her.

"Ms. Nugent's seen too many flips?" Darcy repeated.

"Exactly." Stephanie groaned. "Well, apparently you were wrong, Darcy. Because she wanted to see us all flip our brains out in gym today. My poor bones will never be the same."

Darcy's eyes widened. "Didn't you use a mat?"

"We used them. I just couldn't feel them by the fifth or sixth time I landed on them," Stephanie mumbled. "I guess I did a little more flopping than flipping."

Allie covered her mouth and tried not to laugh.

"It's not funny," Stephanie said. "You're *lucky* Amber isn't in your gym class. Now Ms. Nugent wants to turn us all into gymnasts. And guess who gets to demonstrate?"

"Could it be Amber Armstrong, by any chance?" Darcy asked.

" 'Limber Armstrong' you mean?" Stephanie corrected. "Why, yes, it just so happens."

"Limber Armstrong?" Allie laughed. "You're so funny, Stephanie."

"Speaking of good old Limber." Stephanie nodded to where Amber sat at a table surrounded by Darah Judson, Rene Salter, Alyssa Norman, and some other Flamingoes. "There she is. I thought she said she was busy during lunch."

"She did say she had something to do." Darcy frowned.

"Something to do with people cooler than us, I guess," Stephanie pointed out. "I'm only surprised it took the Flamingoes this long to make her part of their group. Amber sure does look at home with them. You know what they say—birds of a feather flock together."

Amber did look like she belonged in the most popular crowd in school. Her long, layered strawberry blond hair had that perfect windblown look. And she was wearing a white cotton T-shirt with a colorful pair of baggy silk pants cinched at the waist with a woven belt.

"Maybe she's just sitting with them," Allie said. "It doesn't mean she's going to join the Flamingoes or anything."

"Sure," Stephanie joked, lowering her voice to sound like an announcer's. "Will Amber impress the Flamingo judges? She looks cool and confident, and seems to be able to handle the pressure extremely well. No, Amber Armstrong is not going to crack. She wants a good score from the judges and nothing will break her concentration. At the table, the tension is high. Everyone's afraid to breathe as Amber prepares for her performance. Here she goes, she's going to do it: the dangerous Meat-loaf Flip!"

Stephanie, Allie, and Darcy watched as Amber

poked a fork into the slab of meat loaf in front of her, lifted it up, and flipped it back down on her plate.

Allie laughed. "Meat-loaf Flip," she repeated, shaking her head. "What a joker you are, Steph."

"Yeah," Stephanie said. "I should give Joey some new material. I complain about hearing the same old jokes so much—"

Suddenly Stephanie had a great idea.

"That's it!" she cried.

"That's what?" Allie asked, her head cocked.

"My new talent!"

"The Meat-loaf Flip?" Allie asked in bewilderment.

"I didn't know you were looking for a new talent," Darcy said. "Am I missing something?"

"Just a sense of humor," Stephanie teased happily. Stephanie felt better than she had in days. Even Amber Armstrong didn't bother her so much anymore.

"So do you want to go roller blading with us this afternoon?" Darcy asked.

"I'd like to," Stephanie said eagerly, "but I should get home and talk to Joey before everyone else shows up."

"What do you want to talk to him for?" Allie asked. "I thought those dumb jokes of his make you crazy."

"They do!" Stephanie laughed. "But from now on, I'm going to love them."

Allie and Darcy exchanged confused looks.

"I'm going to get pointers from him," Stephanie explained. "To help develop my new talent." She pretended to take a bow. "Darcy and Allie, meet the new Stephanie Tanner—comedienne!"

"Hey, everyone," Stephanie called as she walked in the door of her house that afternoon. "Is Joey home yet?"

Michelle was on the floor, coloring with the twins, and Becky sat on the couch, reading the newspaper.

"Nope," Becky replied. "Not yet. How was school?"

"It was okay, I guess." Stephanie plopped down on the couch next to Becky. A part of her wanted to tell Becky about what had happened with Kyle and how bad she still felt. And Stephanie wished she could confess how envious she'd felt watching Amber in gym. And how hurt she'd been when Darcy and Allie had made such a big fuss over Amber. Becky was always so understanding, and she usually had good advice. But Stephanie couldn't tell her any of it. She'd either sound insanely jealous—or maybe just insane!

43

"Hi, honey, I'm home," Joey joked as he came into the living room from his basement studio. He sat next to Stephanie. The twins crawled over and started untying his shoelaces.

"Joey," Stephanie cried. "Just the person I want to see."

"Well, I'm glad someone wants to see me," he quipped. "Not one club has returned my phone calls all day. I really need to get a gig—and soon!"

"I have a job for you," Stephanie said. She hurried on before she lost her nerve. "I want to be a comic," she told him. "I know I'm funny, but I think I need some coaching. So let's get started. Can you teach me everything you know?"

"That'll take about two minutes," Joey joked. "But seriously, Steph—comedy is hard work. Plus you have to perform really late at night. You still have a bedtime, don't you?"

"Sure, but I don't mean *that* kind of comic," Stephanie explained. "Not a stand-up comic for adults." She paused dramatically. "I want to be a *kids'* comic."

"Comedy for kids?" Joey thought. "Not a bad idea."

"It's a terrific idea!" Becky chimed in. "You do have a great sense of humor, Stephanie," she said. "You show it in your writing all the time."

44

Stephanie winced. *Not lately*, she thought.

"Okay." Joey nodded. "I'll take the gig. And you'll get my best advice. Starting with this—coming up with good jokes is only the beginning," he warned. "You have to concentrate on timing, and how to work the room, and what to do with hecklers when they interrupt your act—and what to do when nobody laughs," he added. "That's the hardest part. *Everybody* bombs sometimes. It's hard to get used to that."

"It still sounds great!" Stephanie cried. "And with your help, I'll be the best kids' comic around!"

Stephanie was so excited about practicing her comedy routine that she was up at the crack of dawn on Thursday, anxious to start—and finish—a day of school. She didn't use all of her allotted three minutes in the shower *and* she even made the early bus!

"Do we get to come watch Club Stephanie?" Darcy asked after Stephanie had finished telling them all about her act.

"Well, not tonight," Stephanie said. "It's my first performance. You guys are my best friends, but I want to try it out on my family first, just in case I really blow it."

"You won't blow it." Allie smiled. "You're too funny."

"And we wouldn't care if you did, anyway," Darcy added.

"I know," Stephanie said. "But if you guys come over, I might get too nervous."

"Call and tell us how it goes," Allie suggested. "I was going to ask you both to hang out at my house tonight. So you can call us there, until nine o'clock."

"Okay," Stephanie said, pulling a paperback book from her bag. "Listen, what do you think of this joke: Why do cows wears bells around their necks?"

"Where did you get that book?" Darcy asked.

"From the library." Stephanie flipped the book shut and showed them the cover: *1001 Jokes for All Occasions.*

"It looks about a million years old," Darcy teased.

"Well, what's the punch line?" Allie asked.

"In case their horns don't work," Stephanie replied. She looked up expectantly.

Darcy and Allie looked dead serious.

"Maybe it's my delivery," Stephanie muttered.

"I think it's the *joke*," Allie suggested. "You're much funnier than that, Stephanie."

"*Much*," Darcy agreed.

46

"You know what?" Stephanie asked, suddenly feeling great. "You're right." She tossed the book back in her bag.

But later that evening as she was finishing dinner, Stephanie wished she still felt as confident as she had that morning. She'd gone over and over the routine she'd written for herself. She thought it went very smoothly, but the closer it came to curtain call, the more nervous she got.

"Attention, attention," Joey said, tapping his glass with a fork. "I have an important announcement to make. We have a very special after-dinner treat. An entertainment extravaganza." Joey hunched his shoulders and slipped into a funny voice. "Presenting the debut appearance of a very *fabulous* performer. I'm *pleased* to announce, *opening* tonight, *Club* Stephanie: starring the one and only *Stephanie Tanner*, a *girl* comic with an *original* shtick—*kid* jokes."

Stephanie began to get a queasy feeling in her stomach.

"Well, I always thought you were funny," Danny said.

Sure, Stephanie thought, *you have to say that. You're my dad.*

After the table was cleared and the dishwasher loaded, everyone gathered in the living room. Joey dimmed the lights and it was time. The opening of Club Stephanie!

Stephanie had decided to make her entrance from the staircase. Jogging onstage was what all the comics and TV hosts did. They always looked very relaxed and in control.

At the top of the staircase Stephanie tried to calm her nerves. After all, this was only her family. They laughed at her all the time, even when she didn't want them to. So what was the difference now?

The difference was that now she was *performing*. Now she was going to see if she had any talent.

Jesse got out his guitar and strummed some introductory chords while everyone settled into place.

Stephanie's hands were shaking, so she took some deep breaths. Then she came down the steps, running like the professional comedians always did.

And tripped on the last step.

Stephanie was mortified, but everyone started laughing. *No, no. Don't laugh at me,* she wanted to say. *That wasn't part of the act!*

"Welcome to Club Stephanie!" she announced instead, jogging to the middle of the living room. Everyone applauded.

"Here's the news from John Muir Middle School," Stephanie began. "Have you noticed the new girl at school? She's a gymnast. Her name is Limber Armstrong.''

Stephanie paused to give everyone time to laugh. Only they didn't. Michelle was the only one who even giggled.

"Well, I saw her in the lunchroom yesterday," Stephanie went on, warming up to it. "She was working out in the corner. She had her lunch on her tray and was practicing"—Stephanie paused for one beat—"the Meat-loaf Flip!''

Michelle rolled over, laughing hysterically. "Meat-loaf Flip!" she cried. "Ha, ha, ha, you're so funny, Stephanie!''

But there was dead silence from the rest of the room.

"After that," Stephanie continued, her throat getting dry, "Limber worked on her ham-springs and her no-handed cart-meals!''

More silence. Club Stephanie was bombing.

Keep going, Stephanie thought, *keep going!*

She tried to remember her next joke, but one look at her audience and she knew it was over. She didn't think they could take anymore. Except for Michelle, of course, who was hooting like an owl.

Joey stood up and pulled her aside. "Listen, kid, I can get you better material.''

Stephanie shook her head. "Let's face it—I'm just not funny. I really bombed.''

"Remember what I told you. It happens to everyone."

"Yeah, but this was the atom bomb," Stephanie said.

"I loved Club Stephanie!" Michelle cried. "Can I bring you in for show-and-tell?"

Great! Stephanie thought. *I'm a hit with the elementary school crowd. Just about the last thing I ever wanted.*

CHAPTER
5

◆　◀　◢　◆

Flopped down on her stomach in bed, Stephanie stared glumly across the room at a loose eye on one of Michelle's stuffed animals. *No Pulitzer Prize,* she thought. *No San Francisco Stompers. And now— no Club Stephanie.*

"Hey, Steph," D.J. said, poking her head into the room. "Don't take it so hard. Club Stephanie was a good idea."

"I don't know what happened, Deej." Stephanie sighed. "The jokes seemed funny when I wrote them."

"I'm sure they did," D.J. agreed. "You're a very funny writer. Probably a better writer than performer."

"Not anymore." Stephanie shook her head. "Everything I do lately comes out wrong."

"What's everything?" D.J. asked, sitting down beside her.

"Writing, music, comedy, gym." Stephanie groaned. "You name it, I can't do it. There's no hope for my future. Not like some people I know."

D.J. looked confused. "And who might these 'some people' be?"

"Oh, no one." Stephanie shook her head. "Especially not the new girl at school." Stephanie flopped over on her back and sighed again. "Her name," she announced, rolling her eyes, "is Amber Armstrong."

"What's so special about her future?" D.J. asked.

"Kyle Sullivan, to begin with," Stephanie blurted. Then she told D.J. all about what happened in the lunchroom, including how she had called Kyle a football. "I thought he was asking me out, but he was really asking Amber out," she wailed.

"Ouch!" D.J. cried. "That must have really hurt."

"Plus she's super pretty, she's got great clothes, and she's also a fantastic gymnast."

"This girl sounds like the one in your Club Stephanie routine," D.J. teased. "Any relation?"

"Yeah," Stephanie admitted, "she's the twin sister."

"Did making fun of her help you feel any better?" D.J. asked.

"I didn't really mean it like that," Stephanie said softly.

"Okay," D.J. said. "But think about this—she might be all the things you say she is, but she's also the new girl in school. Guys always go for that. It's like a big competition between them: which one will she like?"

"She's really cute, Deej."

"Well, you're really cute, too, Steph." D.J. shook her head. "C'mon, don't get down on yourself. How about a new hairstyle to cheer you up?"

"A whole new style?" Stephanie asked nervously.

"How about something less drastic? Something new with your bangs."

"Okay," Stephanie replied. "I can handle that."

Maybe D.J. was right and all she needed was a new look. Stephanie pulled over a chair and went through the huge pile of magazines stacked neatly in her closet. She was supposed to recycle them, but somehow she never got around to it. It looked like she had a year's worth of magazines in there! Stephanie grabbed one and started flipping through it.

Meanwhile D.J. went into her room to get a

comb and her scissors. When she returned, she stood in front of Stephanie and sprayed her bangs with a water bottle and tried combing them in different ways.

"This will be good, Steph," D.J. said. "I promise. See anything in there you like?"

"*Besides* the clothes?" Stephanie asked, turning the pages.

"Any hairstyles that might look good?"

Stephanie shrugged. "If I looked like *these* girls, *any* hairstyle would look good," she muttered. "What do they do, anyway, take gorgeous pills?"

D.J. laughed. "Yeah. Or maybe they overdosed on vitamin G—G for gorgeous, get it?" D.J. asked, nudging her sister.

Stephanie rolled her eyes. "Puh-lease," she said. "One wannabe comedian is all this family can take."

"Okay," D.J. said. "But who are you talking about, you or Joey?"

Stephanie laughed. "Don't let Joey hear you say that."

D.J. began to snip Stephanie's bangs. When she was through, she dried them and smiled. "They look great!"

Suddenly Stephanie screamed and dropped the magazine. "No way!" she said. "I don't believe it!"

"What?" D.J. yelled. "They don't look *that* bad!"

"No, no." Stephanie shook her head "Not the bangs. Her!" She pointed at an ad in the magazine.

" 'Her' who?" D.J. asked in astonishment.

"Amber Armstrong! Who else?"

"She's in the magazine?" D.J. snatched it up and stared at the picture.

"Just look." Stephanie moaned. "She's a model!"

"And talented, too," D.J. reminded her. "Wow."

"Exactly." Stephanie sighed. "I can't believe it! I can't believe she has her photo in *Seventeen* magazine!"

"Well, like you said, she's very pretty."

"I wonder how many other ads she's in!" Stephanie crawled into her closet, tossing shoes and laundry everywhere in her search for another picture of Amber. She frantically flipped through one magazine after another, discarding them outside the closet when she didn't see a picture of the girl.

"There it is!" D.J. suddenly cried.

"Amber? Where? Where?" Stephanie said, looking up at her sister.

"No, Steph. I'm talking abut my blue sweatshirt, the one you borrowed a month ago and neglected to give back to me."

"But I wanted to return it clean."

"When do you plan on doing your laundry again, Steph? The next full moon?"

Stephanie ignored her sister and went back to her search. "I've got to find any other pictures of her," she said. "To show Darcy and Allie."

"Why do you care so much, Stephanie?" D.J. said. "Come on, look in the mirror and tell me you like your hair. I think it looks super."

Stephanie tore her eyes away from the magazines and walked over to the mirror.

"Hey!" she said happily, admiring the layered fringe D.J. had given her. "It does look great, Deej. I love it! Thanks."

"Anytime." D.J. smiled.

"So can I borrow your new red sweater to go with my new hairstyle tomorrow?" Stephanie asked slyly.

"Don't push your luck!" D.J. chuckled. "I don't feel *that* bad for you."

Stephanie gave D.J. a quick hug. As soon as her sister went downstairs, Stephanie pounced on the telephone in D.J.'s room and dialed Allie's number.

"Listen, Allie," Stephanie said as soon as Allie picked up. "Get Darcy on, too. I have something important to tell you! About Amber!"

A moment later she heard Darcy's voice. "What's the hot news?"

"Amber's a model!" Stephanie exploded. "As in fashion model, magazine model, gorgeous model—"

"Steph, slow down," Allie told her. "What are you talking about?"

"Okay, okay." Stephanie took a breath. "I was looking through a *Seventeen* magazine, and there she was, staring right back at me! Amber Armstrong!"

Both girls screamed.

"She's beautiful enough," Darcy said when she was calm.

"I can't believe she's a model," Allie cried. "She never said anything about it!"

"Exactly," Stephanie agreed. "Don't you think it's strange that she's kept this whole thing a secret?"

"Not really," Darcy said. "Maybe she doesn't want to seem like she's bragging or something."

"Yeah," Allie agreed. "Especially being the new girl in school. I think that's nice of her."

Nice of her? Somehow Stephanie didn't think Amber's secret was about being nice. "Don't you think there's something else going on?" Stephanie asked. "What about the way she avoided us today and said she couldn't have lunch with us? And hung out with the Flamingoes instead. Hey—" Stephanie snapped her fingers. "I wonder if *they* know all about her modeling."

"If *they* knew, the whole school would know,"

Darcy reminded her. "You *know* the Flamingoes can't keep a secret."

"True." Then Stephanie said, "If Amber's still modeling, she probably has to go do photo shoots and stuff. Maybe that's why she's always in a hurry."

"She never leaves school early," Allie pointed out. "She's in last-period math class every day."

"But she still seems a little sneaky to me," Stephanie insisted. "Don't you think there must be a reason she hasn't told anyone she's a model?"

"She doesn't know us very well," Allie began. "And she's shy—"

"But is she?" Stephanie interrupted. "Who ever heard of a shy model? You have to stand in front of people all day and let them take your picture! How could she be shy? Didn't you see that performance on the balance beam in front of half the school? I'm telling you, there's a mystery here somewhere."

Over the phone she could hear Darcy and Allie groan.

"Oh, Steph," Darcy said. "Sometimes you have too much imagination!"

Stephanie glanced down at the magazine's cover page. "Wait a second," she said. "This magazine is a year old."

"So what does that mean?" Allie asked.

"I don't know," Stephanie admitted. "But maybe Amber hasn't had a good job in a while and she's embarrassed to admit it. Or maybe she keeps it a secret because something really bad happened to her, or—" Stephanie had to take a breath. She was suddenly so full of possibilities. "Maybe it's not even a picture of Amber. It could be her evil twin sister or something."

"Don't you think you're getting just a little carried away?" Darcy asked.

"Maybe a *little*," Stephanie admitted.

Allie laughed. "Anyway, save the ad and bring it to school tomorrow. Okay? I'm dying to see it!"

"Okay," Stephanie agreed. She hung up the phone and sat staring at Amber's face, which was staring back at her.

I'm sure there's something strange about Amber, she said to herself. She couldn't believe Darcy and Allie didn't agree.

If I was a model in Seventeen *magazine, I wouldn't keep it a secret. There's a story to this,* Stephanie thought. *And I'm going to find out what it is!*

CHAPTER
6

◆ ◀ ◾ ◆

The last thing Stephanie wanted to do on Friday was go to gym class. It was bad enough that this was the day she was supposed to go to the football game with Kyle. She definitely wasn't looking forward to another session of limbering up with Limber.

When Stephanie got there, though, Ms. Nugent was on her way to the nurse's office with some girl from the last class who had bitten through her bottom lip. Ms. Nugent told them they had ten minutes of free time as long as they were doing something athletic and not sitting on the bleachers, gossiping. *Sure*, Stephanie thought, *I'll turn myself into a pretzel, like Amber does when she stretches. No sweat.*

Stephanie left the rest of the class to their basketball drills and decided to get a tumbling mat and try some gymnastics. Maybe she could work some of the soreness out of her muscles that was left over from the other day. She tried a cartwheel and, surprisingly, didn't end up on her rear.

Maybe she'd actually learned something the other day. Maybe all she needed was practice. Stephanie tried another cartwheel and landed cleanly on her feet again.

Hey, she suddenly thought. *I might be good at this after all. Why not?* Maybe, if she practiced, she could get the whole class, or the whole school, or even just Kyle Sullivan to watch *her* on the balance beam someday!

Okay, Stephanie told herself, *a one-handed cartwheel coming up.*

But something folded, or wobbled, or gave out, and the next thing she knew, Stephanie was flat on her back on the mat, feeling sore all over again. She frowned at the gym ceiling, wondering what she had done wrong.

"You threw yourself off by bobbing your head. Try it again and keep your head down this time."

Stephanie sat up, startled. Wasn't everyone busy tossing basketballs on the other side of the gym?

They were. All except Amber.

"Watch me. Keep your eyes on my shoulders and the position of my head," Amber told her, pulling her own mat onto the floor next to Stephanie's.

Stephanie watched while Amber performed a perfect one-handed cartwheel.

Dream on, Steph, she thought. *You'll never be as good as her.* Then for some reason Stephanie was annoyed. She hadn't asked Amber to coach her. And she didn't really want any coaching. Especially not from Amber, the secret magazine model.

"Thanks, but I was just messing around," Stephanie said stiffly.

Amber watched with a puzzled expression as Stephanie stood up, stretched, and walked away. For the rest of the period Stephanie tried to play pickup basketball with some of the girls. But she couldn't keep her eyes off Amber, who was by herself in the corner of the gym, working on her tumbling.

After gym Stephanie showered quickly and rushed to the lunchroom. She was anxious to show Darcy and Allie the *Seventeen* ad. But by the time she got her food, someone else was already sitting in her place.

Amber!

Stephanie couldn't believe that Amber was sitting at her table, with her friends. How could they trust her after she acted so sneaky? And after she lied about being busy for lunch yesterday? Plus Amber liked to keep secrets about herself. Stephanie and her friends told each other everything.

She's a model! Stephanie wanted to scream. *And I'm the only one who knows it!* Stephanie was dying to tell the whole lunchroom Amber's secret. But it was a secret, Stephanie reminded herself. And it would be really mean to tell anyone—except for Darcy and Allie, of course, who already knew. Still, maybe this was her big chance to find out more about Amber's hidden life. Stephanie wasn't a journalist for nothing. Maybe she could write an article for the *Scribe*, the school newspaper.

"Steph," Allie said excitedly. "Amber was just giving us some tips on gymnastics."

"Yeah," Stephanie said. "She gave me some tips in gym, too. And then she did some stuff herself."

Now was her chance. Turning to Amber, Stephanie said, "You held that *one pose* really well. It must take a lot of practice to hold a *pose* like that."

"Um, yes, it does," Amber mumbled, picking at her food.

Darcy shot Stephanie a warning glance.

"What's that?" Stephanie asked innocently, nodding at Amber's lunch.

"A veggie burger," Amber explained. "I'm a vegetarian."

"So you're very *careful* about what you eat?" Stephanie asked. "To keep your *figure?*"

"I guess so," Amber said uncomfortably. "I mean, everyone should eat well."

"Yes, but you're already so slim," Stephanie went on. "You could be a model or something." She ignored Darcy and Allie, who were glaring at her. "Did you ever think about modeling?" she asked.

"Well, I do watch my weight a little," Amber said, avoiding the question. "And I am a vegetarian. But I'm sort of into junk food, too, and—oh, look at the time. Excuse me," she said, standing quickly. "I have to go."

"I can't believe you," Allie said as they watched Amber hurry away.

"What was that, a cross-examination?" Darcy asked.

"What?" Stephanie said. "I asked an innocent question. And got a very sneaky answer."

"Innocent?" Darcy snapped. "You scared her away!"

"But *why* should a question scare her?" Stephanie pointed out. "Unless she has something to hide."

Darcy shook her head. "Let's just see the picture."

"You *did* bring it, didn't you?" Allie asked.

"Picture? What picture? Amber didn't say she was a model," Stephanie teased.

"She didn't say she wasn't," Allie said. "So let's see it."

Stephanie took out the ad and smoothed it open on the table. Darcy and Allie bent over to look. "Yup," they said in unison. "It's her, all right."

"I wonder why she didn't want to tell us," Allie said.

"That's what I meant!" Stephanie cried. "Why did Amber lie? Does she think we aren't cool enough to know or something?"

"I'm sure there's a good reason for this," Allie said. "We just have to get to know her, and it will all come out. I asked her to come over to my house last night," Allie went on.

"You did?" Stephanie asked, surprised.

"Yeah, but she couldn't make it," Darcy said.

"She said she had to go home and start dinner," Allie added. "Her mom's a nurse, and she doesn't get home until late, so Amber cooks dinner."

"Well, don't you think that's strange?" Stephanie said.

"What? That her mom's a nurse?" Allie asked.

"No." Stephanie shook her head. "I mean, Amber's a vegetarian. How long can it take to make salads?"

"Not this again." Darcy groaned. "Stephanie, you've got to stick to the facts."

"Don't tell me you don't think there's something suspicious about her," Stephanie said. "We know she's lying about modeling."

"Or maybe she just doesn't want to tell *us*," Allie suggested. "Maybe she doesn't want to be friends with us."

"Or maybe she doesn't feel comfortable around Stephanie," Darcy said, sitting back.

"What's that supposed to mean?" Stephanie asked.

"Admit it. You're jealous of her," Darcy said calmly.

"Jealous!" Stephanie cried. "Are you kidding?"

"You're still upset about the Kyle thing, aren't you?" Darcy asked, looking at Stephanie closely.

"Of course not," Stephanie said, trying not to blush.

"Are you sure?" Darcy asked. "You seemed upset when we told you we invited her to Allie's house."

"I was busy anyway," Stephanie said.

"Well, are you busy tonight, too?" Allie asked. "Because tonight we thought we'd go to a movie."

Stephanie had to admit it was a fantastic idea. "I'll check the paper and call you before dinner," she said quickly. Maybe it would be good to push away all thoughts of Amber Armstrong and spend some time with her friends.

You're really not jealous of Amber, so don't let her come between you and Darcy and Allie, Stephanie told herself. Because on top of everything else that had gone wrong lately, she couldn't stand it if she started losing her two best friends.

Later that afternoon Stephanie sat on the living-room couch with the portable phone, the receiver jammed under her ear. It was another three-way call.

"I need to think of something big for my next English paper." Stephanie sighed as she turned the pages of the *Chronicle*, the daily paper. "Better than the last one. Our topics are due to the teacher the week after next."

"That's a long way away," Darcy pointed out.

"Yeah, but I need this paper to be great," Stephanie said. "I'd better start doing research this weekend. I want to be really prepared."

"So," Allie interrupted. "What's playing at the mall?"

Stephanie bent over the coffee table and started reading movie ads. "There's the Keanu Reeves movie," she said. "You and I have already seen it three times, Allie, but Darcy has only seen it twice."

Stephanie paused as something caught her eye. "This is it!" she cried suddenly.

"What?" Allie asked. "Is that new Tom Hanks movie opening tonight?"

"No, no," Stephanie said excitedly. "Forget about the movie! You won't believe what I just found!" *Something to make me feel special again!* she thought.

"What is it, already!" Darcy asked impatiently.

"Listen to this." Stephanie read aloud:

"MODELING CONTEST SPONSORED BY NATURAL JEANS
Natural Jeans, as natural as you are!
The Natural Jeans for Teens Company announces its annual modeling contest! Come down the runway in any pair of Natural Jeans. Any shape! Any size! Any style! As long as they're you! If you're our winner, you'll be our model for a year!"

There was silence on the other end of the phone.

"Well," Stephanie said. "What do you think?"

"Are you kidding?" Darcy finally asked. "Modeling? Are you sure this has nothing to do with Amber?"

"Of course not," Stephanie said quickly. "Just because she's a model, does that mean no one else can do it?"

"No," Darcy agreed.

"Huh," Allie said slowly, "can you model?"

"Why not?" Stephanie asked. "I'm very natural."

"Yeah, natural long-lash mascara and natural shade pressed powder," Darcy cracked.

"I meant my *personality* is natural," Stephanie said.

"Like how natural you were when you tried to talk to Kyle?" Allie asked.

"Oh, okay," Stephanie grumbled. "That one time I was nervous. I blew my line. But winning this contest would make up for it. I'd be a natural!"

"*Naturally*," Darcy and Allie said together.

"Come on, are you going to help me or not? We'll all go to the mall tomorrow and buy a pair of Natural Jeans and I'll sign up."

"Are you sure this is what you want?" Allie asked.

"Yeah," Darcy added, "I thought you just said you wanted to spend the weekend doing research for your paper."

"I know, I know," Stephanie said, getting more and more excited. "But I can do that, too. It's still over a week away. And this contest is perfect! Just because Amber keeps *her* modeling a secret doesn't mean *I* have to, too!"

CHAPTER
7

◆ ◀ ◢ ◆

"Well, this is it," Stephanie said the next morning as she and Darcy and Allie stood in the sportswear department on the third floor of the mall's big department store. "And there they are!" Stephanie cried, pointing to the racks of Natural Jeans next to a big poster about the contest.

"Go for it," Darcy said.

"Look." Stephanie excitedly pulled a pair of blue jeans off a rack. "There's a little entry blank attached to the zipper. How cool!"

"What kind of jeans do you want?" Allie asked as all three of them began wading through rows and rows of denim.

"The Naturally Stephanie kind," Darcy joked.

She held up a pair of pink brushed-velvet jeans. "How about these?"

Stephanie shook her head. "Those aren't me," she said. But she wasn't thinking about whether the jeans would look right on her. She was really thinking: What would *Amber Armstrong* wear?

Suddenly she saw a very cute pair of short white denim overalls. She took them off the rack and held them in front of her before a mirror. Looking at her reflection, Stephanie screwed up her face, then shook her head. They were exactly what she would have bought for herself, but she put them back on the rack. *Don't look for what you like*, she thought. *Look for the Amber Armstrong look!*

Allie held up a pair of white jeans with green-and-yellow zigzags. "What about these, then?"

"No, thanks." Stephanie sighed. "I don't want to give the judges a headache."

"These?" Darcy asked doubtfully, holding up a pair of tie-dyed jeans, ripped at the knees.

Stephanie shook her head. "Too retro."

She looked at everything: black jeans with leather pockets, polka-dot jeans, jeans with patches, jeans with extra pockets. After twenty minutes Stephanie was starting to lose hope. And then finally, she found them.

They looked like the American flag. The legs were red-and-white stripes, and all the pockets were blue with white stars. They also looked very tight. But Stephanie could picture Amber wearing them at an Olympic-gold-medal ceremony. They were perfect.

"Be right back," she said, going into a fitting room.

"I hate them," Darcy said when Stephanie came out.

"They're not you," Allie agreed.

"I'll take them," Stephanie said.

The woman at the cash register told Stephanie to go to the fifth-floor register if she wanted to enter the contest.

"Stephanie, don't you think those jeans are a little bit, I don't know . . . loud?" Allie asked as they walked to the escalators.

"And they seem a little tight," Darcy added.

"Trust me," Stephanie said.

When they got upstairs, they saw a big silver-and-blue banner in the middle of the room that read: NATURAL JEANS MODELING CONTEST. Under it was the sign-up desk, with several people sitting around it.

"This is so cool." Stephanie sighed. Then she saw the long line of girls that wrapped halfway

73

around the room. "I guess I wasn't the only one who read the ad," she said, sizing up the competition.

"Uh-oh," Allie said. "You're not going to believe this, but guess who's here."

Stephanie and Darcy watched as Amber Armstrong stepped out of the crowd around the sign-in table. She looked incredible as usual, in a flowered wraparound baby-doll dress over a ribbed T-shirt and a pair of lace-up white leather boots.

"Hey, Amber," Darcy called as she came closer.

Amber looked up and seemed surprised to see them.

"Are you entering the contest?" Stephanie asked. "I thought you said you didn't model."

"Oh, no, I don't . . . I mean, I'm not entering. I came to see a friend." Amber glanced uneasily at the sign-in table.

"Is your friend a model?" Stephanie asked coolly.

"Sort of," Amber admitted. "She's one of the judges."

Stephanie gulped. *Oh, no!* she thought. *What if Amber doesn't want me to win? She could tell her friend not to vote for me!*

"Actually I did meet her while I was modeling," Amber said quickly. "But I've only done a little bit and that was a long time ago, before we moved to San Francisco."

Darcy and Allie looked at Stephanie as if to say, *We told you so. Now there's no more secret.*

"How old were you when you started modeling?" Darcy asked Amber.

"Oh, I can't remember. It was for baby food, I think."

"What was it like?" Allie asked curiously.

"Under all those lights? Hot," Amber answered. "Modeling really sounds like a lot more fun than it is. So why are *you* entering the contest?" she asked Stephanie.

"Uh—I thought I'd try it because, um, sometimes writing gets pretty boring," Stephanie replied.

"Well, it's not as exciting as you might think," Amber said. "Or as easy. But good luck if you're going to try it."

Is she trying to talk me out of it? Stephanie wondered.

"Hey," Allie said, "do you really get to keep the clothes you model?"

"All the time. They're called samples," Amber explained. "In fact, everything I'm wearing is sample stuff. Would you believe that I'm in eighth grade and this is the first year I've ever bought my own clothes? I don't even know what I like anymore," she said, sounding almost sad.

Amber looked at Stephanie. "Are you sure you want to do this?" she asked again.

Stephanie nodded.

"Well, I was a judge at a contest in L.A. once," Amber said. "I helped a girl there and she won. It was a lot of fun. I can give you some pointers, if you want."

"Oh, sure," Stephanie said, feeling a little dazed.

Amber took down Stephanie's address and phone number.

"Steph, that'll be great," Allie said excitedly. "You'll do well if Amber helps you, since she was a model."

"Did I hear you say you were a model?" a voice cried behind them. "Why didn't you tell me, Amber?"

Stephanie, Darcy, Allie, and Amber all turned to see Rene Salter with a pair of hot pink brushed-velvet Natural Jeans slung over her shoulder. Darah and a few other Flamingoes were with her.

Amber shrugged and bit her bottom lip. "That was nice of you to offer to help, Amber," Rene went on, glancing at Stephanie. "Some people need all the help they can get."

Darah and the other Flamingoes giggled. But Amber didn't laugh.

"We missed you at the game on Friday, Amber," Darah said sulkily. "Kyle missed you, too."

"Oh, sorry," Amber mumbled. "I was just really busy last night."

Stephanie, Allie, and Darcy all shared a glance. Was Amber playing hard to get with Kyle? Stephanie wondered. Or was she really busy? Amber really was a mystery.

"So about this modeling thing," Rene went on. "What do you think my chances are of winning?" She paused and looked over at Stephanie and her friends. "I mean, really, the competition isn't that stiff."

"There are lots of pretty girls entering," Amber said.

"May the most beautiful girl win," Rene said.

"I think you mean, the most 'Natural'," Darcy corrected.

"Of course." Rene smiled. "Natural. As in natural born loser." She looked at her friends, and they all laughed.

"Don't listen to her," Darcy said to Stephanie. "She just can't handle all the competition."

Stephanie looked at the long line of girls. *I'm not sure I can either!* she thought.

Stephanie filled out an entry blank and gave it to a very sophisticated woman sitting behind the table. Her blond hair was in a bun, and her makeup was very natural looking.

"This is a live modeling competition," she said to Stephanie. "A runway show. You'll have one rehearsal just before the show. And don't forget to bring a prop."

"What do you mean, prop?" Stephanie asked.

"Something to take down the runway with you," she explained. "Last year our winner came out on a bicycle."

"I get it." Stephanie smiled. "Thanks for the tip."

"Can you believe Rene!" Darcy huffed as Stephanie met her friends at the escalators. "That girl is so stuck up."

"Yeah," Stephanie agreed. "And now Amber's going to help *her* win the contest."

"You don't know that," Allie said. "Amber offered to help you before Rene came over."

"And she did admit that she was a model," Darcy said. "So I guess that means no more secrets, right?"

"*And* she didn't go to the football game," Allie added. "So don't worry, Stephanie."

"She must not like Kyle after all," Darcy said.

"That's even more suspicious," Stephanie muttered.

78

"Stephanie, what's wrong with you?" Darcy said.

Stephanie wasn't sure exactly why she didn't trust Amber, but she just didn't. Would Amber have admitted that she modeled if they hadn't caught her here? And what about the way she talked about modeling, telling Stephanie it wasn't any fun? Was Amber trying to talk her out of entering the contest? And then after everything Amber had said about not liking modeling, why had she offered to help? Maybe she meant to help Rene all along, and she was only trying to sabotage Stephanie's chances?

I have to get some answers, Stephanie thought. *And soon!*

CHAPTER
8

◆ ◀ ◢ ◆

"I've got it!" Stephanie snapped her fingers. It was Monday and she was in the cafeteria with Darcy and Allie.

"You've finally figured out a topic for your English paper?" Allie asked.

"English assignment? Oh, yeah, that," Stephanie said with a wave of her hand. "No, no. But I did come up with a great idea to write about—for the school newspaper. How's this grab you? I'll write an article for the *Scribe* on how it feels to be the new kid in school. And I'll interview Amber."

Amber Armstrong had been on Stephanie's mind all weekend. Stephanie had spent all Sunday looking through old magazines, trying to find more pictures of her. She'd also cut out pictures of natural-looking models. And she hadn't spent even five minutes on her English assignment.

Allie groaned, putting down her turkey sandwich. "I'm getting tired of this subject, Steph."

Just then Stephanie spotted Amber across the cafeteria, sitting alone at a table. A little part of Stephanie had to admit that she felt sorry for Amber, eating all by herself. Then she remembered. *I'm an investigative reporter. And this opportunity is too good to miss.*

"A journalist should stop at nothing to get a good story," Stephanie told her friends, pushing her chair back from the table. "You two can fight over my lunch." Leaving her half-eaten peanut butter sandwich and banana with Darcy and Allie, Stephanie hurried over to Amber's table. "Hey, Amber," she said.

"Hi," Amber answered. "Have you changed your mind about the modeling contest?" she asked, smiling.

"Nope," Stephanie replied. "Did you think I would?"

"I guess not," Amber said. "But I'll still help you if you want."

Before or after you tell all your modeling secrets to Rene? Stephanie almost asked.

"Okay," Stephanie said. "But do you have a minute to talk about something else?"

"Sure," Amber replied, pulling a carrot stick from her bag.

"I'm a reporter for the *Scribe*, the school newspaper," Stephanie began. "And I'm doing an article on new students in school. I'd like to interview you."

"Interview me?" Amber almost choked on her food. She pushed her strawberry blond hair from her shoulders. "Why? About what?"

"Just about you," Stephanie explained. "An introduction to the school. A chance for people to get to know you."

"But there's nothing to get to know."

"Well," Stephanie, noticing Amber's nervousness, "a lot of the kids like to know who the new students are, and not everybody has had a chance to meet you."

Amber began playing with her food, wrapping her carrot sticks tightly in plastic wrap. "I'm really very ordinary."

"I wouldn't say that," Stephanie answered. "Not everybody can do what you did on the balance beam. And it's not exactly ordinary to be a model."

"I'm not a model," Amber said quickly. "Not anymore."

"But you *were*." Stephanie nodded. "That's exciting."

Just then Rene Salter walked by on her way to the Flamingoes' table. She stopped in front of Amber, her back toward Stephanie.

"What's happening, Amber?" Rene said. "Are you giving out more hints for the hopeless?" Rene laughed loudly at her own joke. Amber and Stephanie didn't laugh.

Then Rene said, "Oh, by the way, I meant to tell you, Amber . . ." Rene bent down and whispered something in Amber's ear. Amber listened with a confused look on her face.

When Rene finished, Amber stammered, "Well, yeah, I guess so . . ."

Then Rene said, "Super! I'll see you in math class," and continued on.

Stephanie figured Rene was trying to get more modeling hints out of Amber. She decided to act like it didn't bother her one bit.

"Like I was saying," Amber went on. "Modeling is not all that exciting. I don't think anyone wants to know about it."

"Well, I can think of a few people who do," Stephanie said, glancing over at the Flamingo table. "Anyway, I'm the reporter, remember? Let me be the judge of that."

Stephanie took out her notepad and pencil. "Give me five minutes," she said. "I'll just ask a few questions."

But as Stephanie sat down, Amber stood up. "I'd love to help," she began, "really. But now's not a great time. I have to go. I can't be late." Amber picked up her tray. "Another time?"

"Okay," Stephanie said. "Shall we set a date?"

"Um, sure." Amber shrugged. "But I really have to go now. We can make a date later, okay?"

You mean make a date to make a date? Stephanie almost said. She watched Amber leaving—again. She was getting used to the sight of Amber's back as she ran away.

Stephanie rejoined Allie and Darcy, who were just finishing Stephanie's banana. The first thing she did was tell them about Rene whispering to Amber.

"Oh, whispering in front of other people is so immature," Allie said.

"Sounds just like a Flamingo," Darcy agreed.

"And I bet anything Amber is going to help Rene win that contest," Stephanie said.

"So did your reporting skills put an end to the Amber Armstrong mystery?" Allie asked.

"Not really," Stephanie admitted. "She doesn't think being great at gymnastics and being a model are very interesting. She ran away before I could ask her one question.''

''Oh, well,'' Darcy said, sounding relieved. ''I guess you can't get her to spill the beans.''

''But *we* think modeling is interesting. So let's talk about what we're going to do tonight,'' Allie said.

''Tonight?'' Stephanie asked.

''Tonight,'' Darcy repeated. ''We'll create a whole look for you. It'll be great! On one condition.''

''What's that?'' Stephanie asked.

''No more talking about Amber! Agreed?''

Stephanie smiled happily. ''Agreed!''

That afternoon Darcy, Allie, and Stephanie sat in Stephanie's bedroom, scouring magazines for modeling ideas that Stephanie could use in the Natural Jeans contest. And the very first thing they discussed was Amber.

''I guess you were right about Amber,'' Allie said sadly as she pored over fashion ads. ''I mean about her not helping you win the contest.''

''Really?'' Stephanie asked. ''How do you know?''

''Rene Salter gave her a note during math class. I saw what it said: 'Help me win the contest and you'll be Flamingo #2. After me, of course, Rene.' ''

"See?" Stephanie said, trying to hide her disappointment. "I knew she wouldn't try to help me."

"It's really too bad that she's going to join the Flamingoes," Darcy agreed. "I kind of liked her."

"If she's going to be a Flamingo, she might even try to influence the judges of the contest to vote for Rene," Stephanie said.

"Guys," Darcy said, "we're doing it again. Remember we said no Amber today?"

"Right," Allie agreed, going back to the magazines.

"What about cornrows?" Darcy finally asked. "I can do those, and I bet they'd look really cute on you, Steph."

Stephanie had seen lots of girls with the little braids in their hair, mostly when they came back from a vacation to some exotic island somewhere. They always did look great.

"Okay," Stephanie agreed. "You really don't mind?"

"No, it'll be fun. Sit here and keep your head straight up," Darcy said.

"Do you have anything like this?" Allie asked, holding up a picture of a woman in a little red top. "It would go good with your jeans."

"Ouch," Stephanie answered. Darcy was braiding her hair awfully tight.

"It's worth it, Stephanie," Darcy said. "The tighter they are, the longer they'll stay in."

"I must have a red top somewhere," Stephanie replied.

Allie began braiding the other side of Stephanie's head. "What about platform shoes?" she asked. "All the models are wearing them lately. Turn your head to the side."

Stephanie turned and grimaced as Allie yanked at her hair.

"Well, D.J. has a huge pair of shoes. And a new red T-shirt," Stephanie said. *And she'll never let you borrow them,* she added silently.

"And way-out earrings. And makeup, too," Darcy added.

"Ouch," Stephanie answered. "You mean more than just powder and blush?"

"Absolutely," Darcy said. "You have to wear heavy makeup under the lights. Lights make everyone look really pale."

"I didn't know the natural look was so *complicated,*" Allie murmured.

"Almost done," Darcy said finally. "I'll just put in some barrettes."

"Oh, it looks so great!" Allie cried, clapping. "You're going to love it."

Stephanie kept her eyes shut until Darcy gave her a mirror.

"Steph, open your eyes. You won't believe

this! It looks so cute." Darcy fell back on the bed.

"Wow!" Stephanie said, opening her eyes and blinking. "That's me? Is that really me!"

Her blond hair was evenly and perfectly cornrowed into lots of little braids. Barrettes, like chunks of confetti, were scattered throughout her hair.

"I love it!" Darcy cried.

"Me too!" Allie agreed.

"Me three," Stephanie said, amazed at the difference.

"Well, listen," Darcy said. "I have to go now, but remember, the hair isn't enough. You need the whole outfit: clothes, earrings, shoes, makeup."

"Don't forget I need to work out a dance routine, too," Stephanie said.

"You'll be great," Allie agreed.

Stephanie hardly noticed as they left. There was so much to do! She got out the Natural Jeans she'd bought at the mall and pulled them on. They *were* awfully tight, and she had to jump around in them to get them on.

Now, where was that red T-shirt? She felt sneaky going into D.J.'s closet. But she could ask to borrow it later, when her sister got home. D.J. would understand—it was for one of the most important days in Stephanie's life! Stephanie took the shirt off a hanger. The color was perfect with the jeans.

"Shoes, shoes," she hummed to herself as she plowed through D.J.'s closet. She found the black suede shoes way in the back. *Please, please, give me a break this time, D.J.,* Stephanie silently pleaded.

Now, what about makeup? She didn't think her dad would go for the heavy stuff at all. But Stephanie *had* worn it once for a school play. *He'll understand*, she reassured herself. *After all, he's in the entertainment business.* She slathered a thick coat of foundation on her face, then blusher and lipstick.

Now what? Oh, right—Darcy had said earrings. Rummaging through D.J.'s jewelry box, Stephanie found the perfect pair. They were long and slinky, with silver stars at the ends.

Stephanie finished putting herself together and stepped back to take a look.

"Dinner's on the table, Steph," Danny called up. "It's your favorite, fried chicken and corn on the cob!"

Stephanie barely heard him. She was still staring at herself in the full-length mirror. She'd done everything that Darcy and Allie had suggested, everything that the models in the magazines did. And she looked terrible! Who was that person in the mirror?

When Stephanie had imagined Amber in these jeans, it had seemed to make so much sense. Now, though, Stephanie couldn't picture Amber wearing anything like this at all! Was it the makeup? The earrings? The shoes?

The shoes were hard to walk in, but that would just take practice. So why did the whole thing look so strange?

"Steph," Danny called again. "Honey, we're waiting."

Stephanie panicked. She looked ridiculous, but there was no time to change. She'd just have to make the best of it. Maybe she looked better than she thought. Maybe she just had to get used to her new look.

"Stephanie!" Danny called again.

"I'm coming, I'm coming," she called back. Very, very slowly she walked down the stairs in the platform shoes.

Stephanie took a deep breath. It was now or never.

As she walked into the kitchen, Stephanie could hear the usual dinner noises—chitchat and the clatter of plates and glasses being passed out.

"Hi, everyone!" she said brightly.

Eight faces looked up. All the noise stopped for a moment.

"Honey?" Danny began to say.

"Who's that?" Nicky asked, pointing.

"It's Stephanie," Michelle said, with a puzzled expression. "I didn't know it was Halloween already."

Alex began to cry. "Where's Stephanie?" he wailed.

D.J. burst out laughing.

"I'm sorry I borrowed your stuff without asking," Stephanie started.

"It's not that," D.J. said, trying to catch her breath. "It's the makeup. It has to go. And so do the shoes." She chuckled. "And where *did* you get those jeans?"

"You look weird," Michelle said, dumping mashed potatoes on her plate. "But I like the earrings. I'll give you a quarter for them."

Stephanie's heart sank. Obviously this was *not* an Amber Armstrong outfit. And it sure wasn't a Stephanie Tanner outfit, either.

"Here, sit down, honey," Danny said, filling her plate. "Don't feel bad. You tried a new look and it didn't work. But Steph, can I ask you why you thought you needed to change your style?"

"Dad, I know this isn't really me," Stephanie explained, "but it's for this modeling contest, and I—"

"What modeling contest?" Danny asked, surprised.

"I saw it in the newspaper," Stephanie explained. "It's sponsored by the Natural Jeans Company. The winner gets to be a model for a whole year!"

"Oh, you don't want to do that, Stephanie," Jesse said. "Models don't have a normal life, you know? Like, they can never just hang out with other kids."

"They never get any privacy," Joey said. "Once you get famous, people are always hounding you for your picture and autograph. . . . I should know," he added.

"You wish," Jesse replied.

But Stephanie had her mind set. She looked anxiously at her father. "Well, Dad, can I do it?"

Danny sighed and put his elbows on the table. "I can't make that decision for you, but I hope you consider everything."

"Like what, Dad?" Stephanie asked, dreading the answer.

"Like what will happen if you win the contest? Will modeling get in the way of your schoolwork or your friends? You also have to consider your writing career. But I guess it's your choice," he finished.

"Oh, thank you!" Stephanie leapt up and threw

her arms around him. "Don't worry. If I win, nothing will suffer."

"Except me," Michelle said. "I have to sleep with you in the same room. That hair might give me nightmares!"

"One thing, Stephanie," Becky said. "If you're going to do this, you should find your own style. You're not a cornrow girl. Same for the shoes. And the makeup."

"And the pants," D.J. added with a smirk.

"I agree," Jesse announced. "Anyway, didn't you say it was a natural contest?"

"You're all right," Stephanie mumbled. "This isn't me. And it isn't very natural, either, is it?"

"You just be yourself," Danny answered, giving her shoulder a squeeze. "And everybody will love you just the way we do."

Even the judges? Stephanie wondered.

CHAPTER
9

Stephanie could feel a warm blush spreading over her face from her neck up. Everyone at school was actually turning around to stare at her as she passed. She couldn't really blame them. She felt like she was wearing a mop on her head.

Stephanie had to agree with her family. She wasn't a cornrow person. She'd wanted to take them out last night, but she hadn't had time. So she wore her new look to school. It was like a bad dream.

Just as Stephanie got to the pay phone where Darcy and Allie were waiting, Amber walked right past them, looking perfect in a denim skirt and a cropped linen jacket with big buttons. Just like a model from *Seventeen*.

Good one, Steph. She is *a model from* Seventeen! *How could you forget?*

"Hi, Amber," Darcy and Allie said.

Amber said hello and kept walking. Then abruptly she stopped in her tracks and turned around.

"Stephanie? Is that you?" Amber asked, staring at Stephanie's hair. "What happened to you?"

Automatically Stephanie's hand went to her head. "I'm just trying out a new look," she muttered.

"Well, if you're doing that for the Natural Jeans contest, I think you're making a mistake," Amber said. "Hair like that isn't very natural."

Stephanie knew her hair didn't look very good, but she couldn't help feeling offended by Amber's comment.

"That's just my opinion," Amber added with a shrug.

"And you know all about modeling," Stephanie said.

"Uh . . . well." Amber looked embarrassed.

"Actually I'd like to know more about it," Stephanie said, pretending she hadn't meant to sound nasty. "Maybe we could talk at lunch today. I still want to interview you for the *Scribe*. And then you can give me all the help I need."

"I'm sorry," Amber said. "Today's no good for me. We'll do it some other time, Stephanie. I promise. Bye."

"She did it again!" Stephanie turned to Darcy and Allie. "You saw that, right? She absolutely refuses to talk to me."

"And I absolutely refuse to listen to this anymore," Allie said firmly. "I like Amber."

"It's not that I don't like her!" Stephanie argued. "Anyway, how can you like her when she won't even let you get to know her?"

"All I know is, I don't want to hear anymore about it," Allie said, exasperated.

Stephanie shook her head. Maybe her friends had no curiosity, but Stephanie sure did. Amber Armstrong was too secretive. Something was going on with her, Stephanie was sure of it. Maybe it had to do with the Flamingoes. Maybe they told her not to hang out with Stephanie or her friends. For some reason, Amber didn't want anyone to know too much about her.

But I'm going to find out, Stephanie resolved. *Even if I have to do it all on my own. And I have a perfect idea how!*

When she got home after school, she went to D.J.'s room, where she could talk on the phone without anyone hearing. D.J. wasn't home, so she had the room to herself. *Perfect!* Stephanie thought. *If I can pull this off!*

Stephanie shut the bedroom door. She checked her watch again and went to her phone.

If Amber's mom worked the evening shift, Stephanie should be able to catch her at home before she left. Stephanie was determined to get the information she needed out of *someone*.

But what if Amber answered the phone? Stephanie felt a rush of panic. *Calm down, calm down,* she told herself. All she had to say was, "Is your mother home?" She could do that!

Feeling better, she dialed information and got the number. Then she hesitated for a moment, wondering if she could really go through with her plan. But there was no time to think. D.J. was out of her room now. She had the privacy she needed. She had to act fast. Stephanie dialed.

"Hello?"

Great. It wasn't Amber!

"Is this the Armstrong residence?" Stephanie asked nervously, her voice coming out in a squeak.

"Yes, it is," answered the woman, who had to be Amber's mother. "How may I help you?"

"Well, I'd like to speak to the head of the household, please. This is"—Stephanie glanced at her notes—"the San Francisco Survey Service." Good thing she'd written that out before she dialed! She wasn't a reporter for nothing.

"Yes, this is Mrs. Armstrong."

Stephanie held her breath for a second and then released it. She couldn't believe she was doing this!

"I wonder if you could answer a few questions."

Just then she heard Michelle at the top of the stairs. *If you come in this room now, Michelle, I'll kill you,* she thought. Her palms were sweating so much, she was afraid she might drop the phone.

"How many people in your household, please?" Stephanie asked in her most businesslike tone.

"Two. Just my daughter and myself."

"And, uh, is your daughter an only child?"

"I beg your pardon, where did you say you were from?"

"The San Francisco Survey Service," Stephanie repeated. "We're working on the employment figures in the area."

"Well, I'm working as a nurse right now, if that's what you want to know," Mrs. Armstrong replied.

"And is your daughter also currently working?"

"My daughter has worked as a model in Los Angeles, but now that we've moved to San Francisco, she doesn't work anymore."

"Is she receiving unemployment benefits, then?" Stephanie asked, trying to sound matter-of-fact.

"Oh, no." Mrs. Armstrong chuckled. "She's only fourteen. Fourteen and a half, actually. She's a full-time student."

She's almost fifteen! Stephanie's mind whirled.

"She must be in high school, then," Stephanie squeaked out.

"Well." Mrs. Armstrong sighed. "Actually she *should* be in the ninth grade, but she slipped back a grade in L.A., so . . ." Suddenly Mrs. Armstrong paused. "Uh, excuse me? What did you say your name was? Miss . . . ?"

"Miss Michelle," Stephanie said, saying the first name that came to mind.

Hearing her name, Michelle opened the door and skipped into the room. "What do you want?" she asked.

Stephanie shook her head at Michelle and said "Shhh," with her finger to her lips.

"Yes, well, are these questions really neces-sary—"

"Then why'd you call my name?" Michelle persisted.

"No, no," Stephanie muttered quickly to Mrs. Armstrong. "Thank you very much. One employed adult. Thank you again. Good-bye!"

Stephanie couldn't believe it.

Amber Armstrong the Perfect. With the gorgeous model looks. And the high-fashion wardrobe. The dazzling gymnast.

Amber Armstrong had flunked a grade!

She'd said she wasn't a model. But she was.

She'd pretended she was only thirteen. But she wasn't.

She was nearly fifteen and only in the eighth grade. She was older than some of the ninth graders!

It was unbelievable!

Michelle stood in front of Stephanie, staring at her. Finally she said, "Were you talking to someone named Michelle?"

"No, I was Michelle."

"Does that mean I get to be Stephanie?" Michelle asked, confused.

Wow, Stephanie thought, ignoring her sister. *What will everyone say when they hear this?*

She couldn't wait to spill the beans! Finally she knew Amber's secret—and it was *incredible.* The coolest girl in all of John Muir Middle School had flunked a whole grade!

CHAPTER
10

◆ ◀ ◂ ◆

"I don't believe it," Allie said, leaning against the pay phone. "How could she have flunked? She doesn't seem stupid. And I can't believe she's almost fifteen!"

"Shhh," Stephanie said. All through the hall kids were walking by in little groups. "Look, that's what her mother said. And she ought to know."

"Stephanie, I can't believe you talked to her mother," Darcy said. "How could you play a sneaky trick like that?"

"It wasn't a trick. Reporters always do that stuff."

"It sounds like a trick to me," Darcy said. "You say that Amber's sneaky. Look at you!"

"Amber's still sweet. Even if she did flunk," Allie said.

"And I still think she's cool," Darcy said.

"Wait a second," Allie said thoughtfully. "If she was a model, then maybe that's why she had trouble in school. Don't models have to work all the time?"

"Sure, it must have been really hard," Darcy said.

Stephanie shook her head in frustration. "You're not getting the point. She flunked a grade! She's not perfect. She lied to all of us and that's why she always slinks around acting so secretive. She's afraid we'll find out."

"Well, if I did poorly in school, I wouldn't want everyone in the world to know it," Darcy argued.

"Yeah. I feel sorry for her," Allie said. "She probably has to work really hard just to catch up. Maybe that's why she's always busy. She must have to study all the time."

"I can't believe you tricked her *mother*," Darcy muttered.

For a moment Stephanie felt really guilty. Her friends were making her feel like she did a terrible thing. It didn't seem right. After all, Amber had snubbed them and was now hanging out with the Flamingoes. Why was Stephanie all of a sudden the bad guy?

As if Stephanie had conjured her up just by thinking, Amber passed by in pink thigh-high stockings, big black shoes, a small baby-doll white T-shirt, a pink vest . . . and a pink skirt with buttons up the front. The skirt looked like it was made out of vinyl. Amber looked unbelieveable.

Everyone was watching her as she walked down the hall. Incredibly she had an innocent look about her, like she had no idea what a sensation she was causing. *But she must know*, Stephanie thought. *It has to be an act. Models learn to do that on the runway.*

Stephanie watched as Amber passed by a small knot of Flamingoes, including Rene and Darah. They took one look at her, smiled, and gathered around her like a flock of birds.

"Oh, I get it!" Stephanie said to Darcy and Allie. "Amber is wearing pink today. That must mean she's definitely going to be a Flamingo after all."

"You must be right," Allie said sadly.

"Too bad." Darcy shook her head.

Stephanie's heart sank. So much for the contest, she thought. Now she had no chance of winning. Not if Amber was going to be helping Rene.

When she got home from school, Stephanie dragged the coffee table over against one wall.

Becky walked into the living room and asked what she was doing.

"Trying to clear a space so I can practice my dance routine," Stephanie explained. "The one I'm doing for the Natural Jeans contest. I'm using my Walkman as a prop, when I dance down the runway. But I need to work out some moves, 'cause the contest is this Saturday."

"Good idea," Becky agreed, heading for the kitchen just as the doorbell rang.

"I'll get it," Stephanie called. She ran to the door and pulled it open. And froze.

"Amber," Stephanie choked out. "Uh—hello."

"Hi!" Amber said brightly, her red-blond hair glinting in the afternoon sun. "I came by to help you with the contest." She looked over Stephanie's shoulder. "Is now a good time?"

Stephanie stood staring for what felt like hours. She was so surprised she couldn't move. "I didn't expect to see you," she finally admitted.

"I know," Amber said apologetically. "I'm usually really busy. But I did say I'd help you, and if you really want to be a model, I might be able to give you some good advice."

Stephanie didn't know what to do. She'd thought for sure that since Amber had joined the Flamingoes, she'd never give Stephanie any help.

Unless Amber was here on a Flamingo mission, Stephanie thought.

Maybe the Flamingoes put her up to it, to give Stephanie really bad advice so she'd be sure to lose! Or maybe they sent Amber over as a spy to find out what Stephanie was wearing and using for a prop.

Stephanie glanced down at Amber and noticed that she wasn't wearing her pink ensemble. "Oh, I see you changed," Stephanie said.

Amber looked down at her baggy jeans, white T-shirt, and black sneakers. "That pink outfit was a bit silly, wasn't it?" she sighed.

"Silly?" Stephanie gasped. "You looked amazing!"

"Really?" Amber asked, acting genuinely surprised. "I've spent so many years wearing other people's clothes and styles that I don't have any idea what looks good on me. Or what I like."

I can't believe that Amber has no idea how great she always looks, Stephanie thought.

"Still, I don't think I'm going to wear that outfit again." Amber shrugged. "Especially the skirt."

"But it's pink!" Stephanie cried. How could Amber be a Flamingo if she didn't wear pink?

"But I hate pink." Amber sighed again. "Even though it seems to be a pretty popular color at school these days."

Stephanie was dying to ask Amber if the Flamingoes knew how she felt about the color. But she thought it might be best not to bring them up.

"After so many years working with people who could only talk about clothes," Amber went on, "it's one of those things I almost never look at. I really don't care. I'm just trying to figure out what's comfortable and what makes me feel good about myself.

"Anyway, let's get down to business." Amber smiled. "Do I have to spend all afternoon on your front step, or do I get to come inside?"

"I'm sorry, of course you can come in," Stephanie cried, opening the door wider so Amber could get by. She still couldn't believe that Amber was here to help, but she seemed sincere. Stephanie decided to be on her guard.

"Wow, you really have a big house," Amber said, standing in the middle of the living room. "My mom and I live in a tiny apartment. How many people are in your family?"

"Nine," Stephanie said. "It's an unusual household. We're sort of an extended family."

"So," Amber asked, "you've already bought your jeans?"

"Let me get them," Stephanie said. "They're so cool!"

Stephanie ran upstairs. She was back in a flash with her stars-and-stripes Natural Jeans and held them up for Amber to see.

Amber looked very surprised. "Wow!" she said. "Can I ask you why you picked those?"

Stephanie wasn't sure how to answer. She couldn't very well tell the truth: *Gee, Amber, I imagined you wearing them and getting a gold medal at the Olympics.*

"Never mind," Amber said, seeing Stephanie hesitate. "But I don't think the judges will go for those."

Stephanie started to panic.

"It's not a Fourth of July parade," Amber said kindly. "And those jeans aren't you at all. You're smart and funny and full of personality. You need something that says that."

Stephanie almost choked. Amber thought she was all those things?

"There's really only one trick that's successful in modeling," Amber said, suddenly serious and businesslike.

"What is it?" Stephanie asked, holding her breath.

"Be yourself," Amber replied. "It may not sound like much, but it is. Be yourself. Be natural. Everything you do should be your own personality."

"That's what my family keeps saying," Stephanie admitted.

"Were there any other Natural Jeans that you liked when you were shopping the other day?" Amber asked.

"Well, yeah," Stephanie said, thinking of the overalls she'd wanted to buy. "There *was* this other pair I liked."

"And I bet they weren't pink brushed velvet," Amber said with a sly smile.

"Nope," Stephanie agreed. "They were actually shorts. White overall shorts."

"You're kidding!" Amber said excitedly. "That sounds perfect! Exactly what I would have thought for you. Casual and fun, with a sense of humor."

Stephanie couldn't help feeling flattered.

"Can you still exchange those?" Amber asked, looking at the crumpled pile of red, white, and blue denim on the couch.

"They did say exchange within seven days." Stephanie smiled. "So they're really that bad, huh?"

Amber just grinned.

"At least you're diplomatic." Stephanie nodded. "Allie and Darcy told me they hated them."

"Well, I'm sure this other pair you mentioned will be perfect, if you can get them."

"I'll get them," Stephanie said. "Maybe D.J. can drive me over later this afternoon."

"You're so lucky to have such a big family," Amber said wistfully. "Sometimes it gets boring with just two people."

"Yeah, but you probably have your own room," Stephanie said. "I hate sharing a room with my sister Michelle."

"I wish I had a sister," Amber said. "My parents were divorced when I was only one. And I don't see much of my dad."

"That's too bad." Stephanie shook her head. She understood how it was to miss a parent.

"Yeah. I mean, I really love my mom, but if I hadn't gotten out of modeling, she would have had me auditioning for movies next!"

"And that's bad?" Stephanie couldn't help asking.

"It wasn't what I wanted."

"Well, what did you want?" Stephanie asked.

"I wanted to be a gymnast. That's probably no surprise," Amber said. "But you have to spend so many hours practicing. There wasn't time to do both."

"Wow," Stephanie said. "But wasn't modeling exciting?"

"At first it was," Amber admitted. "But mostly it was hard work. I really missed out on my childhood." Amber shrugged. "It looks glamorous and exciting from the outside. But from the inside, it's not such a nice job. You wouldn't understand unless you'd been through it."

"That's hard to believe," Stephanie said. She couldn't help wondering if Amber was really telling her the truth. How could modeling not be great? Everyone thought Amber was so special, and she was a model.

"Well, it's different for everyone," Amber said. "Maybe you'll love modeling."

"I hope so," Stephanie admitted. "Because right now, I really want to win that contest."

Just then Comet lumbered into the living room and padded over to Stephanie, poking his wet nose into her hand for a treat. Stephanie patted his head absentmindedly and then pushed him away. But Comet wasn't willing to give up so easily, and he trotted over to Amber.

"Hey, Stephanie," Amber suddenly said, her eyes bright with excitement. "I've got a great idea for the prop for your routine."

"Really?" Stephanie asked. "Better than a Walkman?"

"You can keep the Walkman," Amber said. "But I've got something else in mind. It could blow everyone's socks off."

"Well, what is it?" Stephanie asked excitedly.

"You'll never believe me when I tell you," Amber cried.

Stephanie had to admit that Amber seemed genuinely eager to help her. Stephanie also had to admit that the more she talked to Amber, the more she realized that Amber was a really nice person. Not all that secretive or snobby, just a little shy and unsure of herself. Which was really weird coming from the girl who seemed to have everything.

"So tell me, what's your idea?" Stephanie asked Amber.

Amber began explaining, and Stephanie found herself listening eagerly.

And when Amber was finished, Stephanie realized that she was right—this was a really great idea!

CHAPTER
11

◆ ◀ ◾ ◆

Finally it was the big day! Stephanie had practiced hard every day after school, but she still was so nervous her stomach felt like it was tied in a knot.

The big auditorium in the mall had been transformed for the Natural Jeans contest. A long runway took up the center of the room. Spotlights whirled over the walls. Huge streamers hung above rows and rows of folding chairs. Everywhere were ushers wearing Natural Jeans pants with white T-shirts that said AS NATURAL AS YOU ARE in big letters.

As soon as Stephanie walked through the dressing-room door, she felt like a real model. Above each dressing table there was an oval mirror surrounded by bright, shiny lightbulbs. A woman with a clipboard checked off Stephanie's name and showed her to her own table.

Stephanie put down her small bag and sat on the stool. She stared into the mirror and remembered Amber's advice. No heavy makeup. The judges might disqualify her if it didn't look right. She took out some light powder and dusted her cheeks, nose, and chin to keep the lights from making her face look shiny.

A man in a purple sweatshirt blew the whistle hanging around his neck. "I'm Steve, the stage manager. Time for the run-through, everyone!" he called.

Steve had all the girls line up outside the dressing room. The curtains were pulled closed in front of the stage, so they couldn't see the audience or the runway.

"For now, you'll walk across the stage. No props," Steve told them. "Just once across, take a turn, and back again. Nice and easy. Remember to smile!"

He patted the first girl on her shoulder and sent her out. Stephanie watched three girls go before her, and then it was her turn. She took a deep breath, then hurried across the stage, trying to walk naturally. At the far side she turned, smiled at the imaginary audience, and hurried back.

"Good job," Steve told her. "Now back in the dressing room and get ready for the real thing."

Stephanie already felt like a star. No doubt about it, she already loved modeling. It was exciting and glamorous. Obviously Amber had only seen the bad side of it.

Stephanie finished her makeup, then turned to inspect her competition. She was shocked. All the other girls had awesome outfits on. There were gold jeans with chains. Fire engine red jeans. Even yellow leather ones!

Oh, no, Stephanie thought. *What if Amber was wrong about my outfit!*

Stephanie had chosen a red T-shirt and black high-top sneakers to go with the white overall shorts. She didn't look like anyone else, and she hoped that was a good thing.

Stephanie crossed the room and looked at herself in a full-length mirror. Turning around to get all angles, she frowned. These were the jeans she really liked, she reminded herself. And Amber had told her to be herself.

But had Amber given her the right advice? She had been surrounded by Flamingoes all week in school, and Rene never seemed to leave her side.

Stephanie knew Rene would do anything to win this contest. Darcy had heard her in the girls' room asking Amber questions about the judges for the contest. Had Rene convinced Amber to talk to the judges and try to get them to vote for her?

Just then a girl came up behind Stephanie and tried to get a look at herself in the mirror. She was wearing purple jeans and a big floppy hat. She looked really cute, Stephanie thought. Then she noticed that the girl was also eyeing Stephanie's outfit very closely.

Stephanie felt the tension in the room rising. Everyone was smiling at everyone else, but privately the girls were sizing each other up. The competition had already begun, even before the show started! And it was making Stephanie even more nervous than she already was.

Maybe this is what Amber was talking about, Stephanie thought briefly.

Stephanie slipped out of the dressing room and took a peek through the velvet curtain. She was shocked by what she saw. The auditorium was packed! Somehow she hadn't expected so many people, so many faces staring up at her. Then on the right, in the front row, she saw Darcy and Allie, whispering about something, and the rest of her family. She watched them for a moment. Michelle and the twins were squirming around, and Danny was telling some very long and boring story to D.J., who looked like she was falling asleep. Becky and Jesse were looking at their programs. The only one missing was Joey. He was waiting near the entrance to the dressing room with her prop.

Stephanie took a deep breath and tried to calm herself. Looking out at her friends and family, she wished for a moment that she were safe in the audience with them.

"I'm sorry, miss, you can't stand there," the stage manager said. "This way has to be clear for the contestants."

Stephanie decided it was time to find Joey and get her prop. She found him just outside the dressing room, standing there patiently.

"You'll be fine, Stephanie, I'm sure of it," Joey said when he saw her.

Stephanie took her prop and said, "Wish me luck."

"Break a leg, kid," Joey said, giving her a hug.

"Okay, if I don't have a heart attack first."

Back inside Stephanie heard Steve's voice call out, "Okay, ladies. Now listen up. I'm going to give you your numbers and you can line up with your props behind the curtain."

"This is it," Stephanie said to herself.

Suddenly a snooty voice behind Stephanie said, "I can't believe you brought your dog with you."

Stephanie turned around, although she'd know that voice anywhere. It was Rene Salter, in her hot pink pants.

"If you must know," Stephanie replied, "Comet is my prop."

"Really?" Rene looked troubled. "Did you check with the judges? I'm positive that 'props' are supposed to be things—not pets. You'd better leave him here. You could get thrown out of the contest."

Stephanie's jaw dropped. Was that true? Why hadn't anyone else told her?

"Actually, Rene, they've always let contestants use animals, if they're original enough to think of it." Stephanie looked to her right and saw Amber beside her, smiling sweetly at Rene. Stephanie couldn't believe that Amber had actually stuck up for her in front of Rene. Flamingoes never did things like that!

"Well, then." Rene smiled. "Lucky for you, I guess." She slid into the crowd of girls.

"That helped," Stephanie said to Amber.

"Hey, Stephanie," Amber said. "You look great. Just wanted to wish you luck."

"Thanks," Stephanie said, thinking about Rene. *What a dirty trick she tried to pull.*

"Anyway," Amber said. "Are you and Comet ready?"

"We practiced all week," Stephanie replied. "We'd better be!" Just then Comet whimpered. He wasn't used to being on a leash for too long. Stephanie gave him a dog biscuit, one of several she'd thought to stick in her pockets earlier.

"I'd better get going," Amber said. "Good luck."

Steve read off the names. "Anne Marie Sabatini. Rene Salter. Dawn Frank. Cindy Peters. Jessie Rivera. Beth Fishbein. Stephanie Tanner . . ."

"That's me!" Stephanie said. She was so excited, she jumped up and ran to the door.

"Okay, get in line," Steve said.

This was it! In a minute she would walk the runway like a real model!

"Now," Steve said, going down the line, "when I tap you on the shoulder, you do your thing. Keep it simple and remember . . ." He smiled widely. "Be as natural as you are."

Some taped music started. Stephanie could see the runway from her position in the lineup. The first girl was wearing bright green jeans with a diamond pattern. As she walked, she expertly worked a bright green yo-yo. The yo-yo was glowing. What a great prop! Stephanie couldn't take her eyes off it. This girl was really good—and she knew it. Stephanie could tell from the way she smiled at the crowd.

Stephanie began to feel more nervous. She reached down and patted Comet, who stood perfectly still beside her.

Rene sauntered down the runway next, tossing flower petals from a basket and blowing kisses. Stephanie noticed she hadn't really tried for a natural look. She had more makeup on than the other girls, and her hair was stiff with hairspray. But Stephanie had to admit that Rene really shined onstage. It was clear that she loved all the attention. Maybe her look *was* what was natural for her.

Then there was a girl with a stuffed animal. The next one held an umbrella. Then a girl with a tennis racket, then one with a smock and a fistful of paintbrushes—

Suddenly Stephanie felt a tap on her shoulder.

It was her turn!

She patted Comet's head and held his leash tightly.

"Good boy, Comet, good boy," Stephanie whispered, her voice shaking.

This was it!

The curtain opened to let them through. Stephanie blinked. Big spotlights were shining right in her eyes. She blinked again.

"Good boy, good boy," she murmured to Comet. Smiling, Stephanie started her dance routine. She was holding her Walkman with one hand and Comet's leash with another. It was all happening so fast!

But she could feel the audience with her. She could even hear a smattering of applause.

Then she felt a tug on the leash and heard a low growl.

"Not now, Comet," she whispered, trying to keep a smile plastered on her face. He growled again.

"Behave!" she said through clenched teeth. "I swear, there's more Dog Yummies in it for you." She hoped Comet understood what a bribe was.

But in a few seconds she realized he didn't. Comet suddenly stopped. He wouldn't move forward. Stephanie tugged on his leash with both hands, trying not to drop her Walkman as she dragged him down the runway.

Suddenly from the audience the twins started waving and shouting, "Comet! Come on, boy! Good doggie!"

Before Stephanie realized what was happening, Comet bolted. With a rush of energy he tore the leash from her hands. Her Walkman flew into the air and smashed on the runway.

"Go, Comet, go!" Stephanie heard the twins shouting.

Comet took off down the runway. Stephanie stood, frozen in horror, as the dog reached the end of the ramp and leapt right off the stage!

Barking madly, he jumped into the first row, where her family was sitting. He climbed from lap to lap, licking everyone's faces.

The entire audience was laughing and clapping. To Stephanie, it sounded like they were laughing at her.

Her act was ruined!

Tears welled up in the back of her eyes. "Comet!" she cried, but the dog stared back at her and yelped.

That made the audience laugh even harder. Stephanie turned around and saw that the other contestants were peeking through the curtain and giggling.

Meanwhile Steve was motioning to her wildly, shouting directions. "Walk down! Finish! Smile and walk back—NATURALLY!"

But it was too much for Stephanie.

She looked at her feet. Her Walkman lay in pieces. She bent down and tried to fit it back together, but her hands were shaking too hard.

She managed to grab the batteries rolling across the ramp. She shoved them into the pockets of her overalls. The whole time, she could hear more laughter coming from the audience.

With her head hanging, Stephanie ran back up the runway, brushing past the other contestants and dashing toward the dressing room.

What a total disaster!

She couldn't believe it! She wished it were all a bad dream. But she knew it wasn't. After all her hard work, everything had gone wrong!

CHAPTER
12

◆ ◀ ▮ ◆

"I can't believe Rene Salter won the contest." Stephanie groaned. "That's all she's going to talk about for the rest of her life."

"Now, Stephanie, is that fair? You were talking about the contest nonstop yourself," Becky reminded her gently.

Stephanie sighed. "After all I went through, it didn't matter what I wore. All anyone saw was that shaggy mutt flying through the air."

"That's why his name is Comet," D.J. teased on her way out of the kitchen.

"Stephanie, you shouldn't let what happened today get you down." Danny put his arm around her shoulders.

"But it was so embarrassing," Stephanie said, raising her head and sighing. "I was totally humiliated."

"People forget, sweetie," Danny assured her. "No one else will think about it even half as much as you do."

"That's right," Allie said. "I've already forgotten the whole thing."

"Me too," Darcy agreed. "I don't remember your dog getting loose or your Walkman breaking."

Stephanie looked at her friends, who'd come back home with her after the contest. "I'm sure you mean to cheer me up," she said. "But it's not working."

"Steph," D.J. called, "someone's here to see you."

Stephanie, Darcy, and Allie went into the living room. Amber Armstrong was waiting for them.

"Hi, Amber," Stephanie said, surprised.

"I just came by to say I'm sorry," Amber began, nervously digging her hands into her jacket pockets.

"Sorry for what?" Stephanie asked.

"Well, I was the one who suggested Comet," she began.

"That's not your fault," Stephanie said. "It was a great idea. Comet just wasn't as interested in being a model as I was."

"You're not mad?" Amber asked.

"No." Stephanie shook her head as she thought about it. "Not anymore. Modeling wasn't as glamorous as I thought," she admitted. "It was very tense. And a lot of hard work."

"I could have told you that," Amber said.

"You did," Darcy reminded her.

"I just wasn't listening," Stephanie said. "But I learned my lesson. It was exciting at first, but then it got really competitive and nerve-wracking."

"Are you positive you're not upset?" Amber asked.

"Nope," Stephanie said—and she really meant it.

Amber gave a sigh of relief. "Now you know why I don't like to talk about being a model," she said. "People can't understand why I quit."

"I understand now!" Stephanie said.

"But most girls don't," Amber said. "You had a chance to try it yourself, so you know. But everyone else is still jealous of me."

Allie and Darcy gave Stephanie a knowing look. Stephanie felt a pang of guilt. "Well, you can't blame them. Look how the boys act around you," Stephanie blurted.

"Like Kyle, you mean?" Amber nodded. "Most guys ask me out before they even know me. That's not really all that flattering."

125

"Sometimes even *smart* people can't see below the surface," Darcy said meaningfully.

"Yeah," Stephanie agreed. "And I should know. I was one of the people who was jealous of you."

There! I said it, Stephanie thought. *I admitted the worst.* But suddenly Stephanie felt much better. About Amber, and about herself.

"I should tell you something else, too," Stephanie continued, since it was time to come clean. "I know you flunked a grade, Amber. I called your mom."

"Yeah," Amber replied, not acting very surprised. "My mom thought there was something fishy about that call. She thought it might be someone from school. I'm glad it was you, though. I've been waiting for someone to say something."

"I didn't tell anyone—except Darcy and Allie," Stephanie said quickly.

"But we won't tell anyone," Allie assured her.

"That's why I'm glad it was you," Amber said. "Someone else probably would have told the whole school. But actually, I was almost happy when I thought my secret was out. It's too hard being sneaky all the time. Now I just might tell everyone myself. Or else I'll let you interview me for the *Scribe*," she teased Stephanie. "Anyway, the reason I don't ever hang out is because I'm being tutored so much. I was afraid if you knew, you'd think I was just stupid."

"Amber," Stephanie exclaimed, "if you need extra help with school, who cares? I'll help you anytime you want."

"Really, Stephanie?" Amber asked. "Because there is something I could use your help with."

"Anything," Stephanie replied. "I owe you one."

Amber looked embarrassed. "Would you help me with my big English paper?"

"Oh, no!" Stephanie smacked herself in the head. Her paper! She was supposed to have a topic for it this coming week. She'd completely forgotten about it. Actually she'd blown it off because she thought modeling would be her new career.

"English hasn't been my best subject lately," Stephanie admitted.

"Really? Ms. Simms told me you're the best writer in our whole class," Amber said.

"She did?" Stephanie was surprised. After the grade she'd gotten, she was sure that Ms. Simms didn't think she was any good at all. Maybe it really was just a matter of putting in the time and working hard. Even if writing was a talent, she still had to be serious about it.

"Well," Stephanie said slowly, "they say you should always write about what you know."

"What do I know about?" Amber sighed.

"Why don't you write about what it feels like to be an ex-model!" Stephanie suggested. "You know, about how people are jealous of you. And how people treat you differently when they know you're a model."

"Yeah, people like Rene Salter," Amber said thoughtfully. "That's not a bad idea."

"What about Rene Salter?" Darcy said curiously.

"Well, ever since word got out that I was a model," Amber said, "Rene sort of glommed onto me. She just wouldn't leave me alone. She wanted all kinds of advice about modeling. I didn't mind telling her what I know, but then she wanted me to join that silly club, the Flamingoes."

"So are you a Flamingo now?" Stephanie said.

"No way," Amber said. "Why would I want to join that club? You know I hate to wear pink!"

Stephanie, Allie, and Darcy all laughed. But Stephanie couldn't believe what she was hearing. All along she'd thought Amber was a Flamingo.

"But why didn't you join?" Stephanie asked.

"I guess I just don't want to get involved with anything that snobby, you know? I mean, people think that models are in some sort of exclusive club. But they're just real people."

"We thought all along that you were a Flamingo," Darcy admitted.

"Yeah, and we thought maybe you would convince the judges to vote for Rene," Stephanie confessed.

"We're sure glad you're not a Flamingo," Allie said with relief.

"No way!" Amber said. "And you know why I'd never want to convince those judges to vote for Rene?"

"Why?" the girls asked at once.

" 'Cause those were the grossest pink pants I've ever seen in my life!"

Darcy, Amber, and Allie had only been gone a minute when the front doorbell rang again. Stephanie and the rest of the family were in the kitchen eating ice cream. They even gave Comet a little ice cream with his biscuits, to calm him down after his upsetting stage debut.

"Dad?" D.J.'s voice called from the living room. "You'd better come out here. There's someone at the door from the Natural Jeans Company. And she wants to talk to you!"

Stephanie's jaw dropped. "Oh, my gosh," she whispered. A smile slowly stretched across her face. "They must be here to see me. Maybe I won second prize or something," she said.

Danny put a hand on Stephanie's arm. "Let's see what this is about before you get excited."

D.J. was standing uncertainly next to their visitor, an attractive older woman with jet black hair, dressed in a sleek black jacket over a shimmering metallic silk skirt. A long necklace with big silver beads hung around her neck. She looked like *she* just stepped off a fashion runway!

"I'm Madeline Morris from Natural Jeans," she said in a husky voice. She held out her hand. "Are you Mr. Tanner?"

Stephanie stepped quickly in front of her father and took Ms. Morris's hand. "I'm Stephanie Tanner," she said. "Welcome to our natural house. Can I offer you anything to drink? Natural spring water? Or anything to eat? We happen to have some chocolate chip cookies, and I can assure you that the chocolate is all natural."

"No, thank you," Madeline Morris said to Stephanie. "I don't have much time. I'm here to discuss business."

"I'm not sure that I want Stephanie to model," Danny said as he shook Ms. Morris's hand.

"Dad!" Stephanie cried.

"Oh, I'm so sorry," Madeline Morris said, "I see there's some confusion. But you don't have to worry, Mr. Tanner. I didn't come here about Stephanie."

Stephanie's heart sank. "You didn't?"

"I don't understand," Danny replied, shaking his head. "What can we do for you, then?"

"It's the dog we want," Madeline Morris said. "May I ask his name?"

Suddenly Stephanie found herself sitting. Luckily she'd been near a chair, because her legs had just collapsed. She put her hands on her stomach. She felt like she'd just been kicked.

Madeline Morris had come for *Comet!*

"Comet?" Becky and Jesse said.

"Comet?" Danny echoed.

"Yes. Who is his owner, exactly?" Madeline Morris asked.

"We all are. He didn't do any damage at the contest, did he?" Danny asked nervously.

"No, no," Ms. Morris said quickly. "He's wonderful! So natural. He really stole the show, you know. People couldn't stop talking about him. Now, what we had in mind was to start with print ads, and then move into TV commercials."

Stephanie covered her eyes with her hands. She just couldn't be hearing this! What would the kids at school say?

Remember Stephanie Tanner and how she lost that modeling contest? First her dog jumped off the stage and then she tripped over her Walkman and couldn't put it back together again. But do you know the really funny part?

They gave the *dog* the modeling contract!

Suddenly Comet ambled into the living room, goofy and innocent as ever. He had no idea that his life had changed.

"Well, there he is now!" Madeline Morris smiled. "Our little star!"

Without any prompting, Comet went right over to her. It was as if she had a Dog Yummie in her fist for him.

This can't be happening, Stephanie thought.

"What's going on?" Michelle came into the room after Comet. Joey was right behind her.

"Something exciting, dear," Ms. Morris explained. "We're here to put Comet on TV! How would you feel about having a famous dog?"

I don't know, Stephanie almost said. *How would it feel to die of embarrassment?*

To her surprise, Michelle frowned. "Wouldn't he have to be away from home a lot?" she asked.

"Some of the time, yes," Ms. Morris admitted. "But he would make a *lot* of money." She turned to Danny. "Well, what do you say, Mr. Tanner? You could put all your daughters through college on the money Comet would earn. And dogs enjoy being the center of attention, don't you think?"

Danny shook his head. "I think we need to have a family meeting about this."

"I understand," Ms. Morris said. "Here's my card. Call me with your decision. But try to make it soon. I don't think you'll get another offer like this one. We're prepared to pay top dollar for this dog. I'll be in touch."

"Don't call us. We'll call you," Jesse said before he shut the door behind Ms. Morris.

As soon as Ms. Morris left, Michelle burst into tears. "I don't want to lose Comet," she cried.

The twins quickly joined in. "No more Comet!" they started to wail.

"Now wait a second, everyone calm down. Nothing's been decided yet," Danny said. "We have a lot to discuss."

"Think about it," Joey offered. "Comet could make a fortune—and he doesn't even have an act!"

"Yeah, but modeling is work, even for animals," Becky said. "And one of us would always have to be with him."

"Okay, okay," Danny said. "The issue here is whether he should do it or not."

"But he does what we tell him to," D.J. pointed out.

Stephanie thought about her humiliating experience on the runway with Comet. Would Comet

133

like being a model dog? He sure hadn't liked being tied up on that leash and stuck under all those hot lights. And poor Comet was just a dog. If he was miserable, he wouldn't be able to say anything. What could he do? Refuse his Dog Yummies?

Stephanie knew without a doubt what her answer to the question was. She shot up her hand and cried, "Well, I vote absolutely, positively, no way should Comet model!"

Danny looked at Stephanie carefully. "Honey, aren't you the one who wanted to win a modeling contest?"

"Yes," Stephanie admitted. "And I'm the one who was onstage with Comet. It was awful. You saw what happened. He hated it." Stephanie paused. "And I didn't like it much, either," she added honestly.

Everyone looked down at Comet, lying on his side with his paws over his ears.

Danny sighed. "Oh, Comet. You were almost a star."

"Right," Joey said. "Now you'll never be more famous than Lassie."

"But he'll still be a part of our family—and that's enough, right?" Stephanie looked at everyone and smiled.

"Right!" Becky shouted.

"So it's settled, then?" Danny asked.

Everyone nodded.

"Yay!" Stephanie cried. "Comet stays right here!"

"Yep." Joey sighed, reaching down to rub Comet behind the ears. "Modeling may be okay for some, but I wouldn't wish it on a dog!"

Suddenly as Stephanie looked around the room a great idea came to her. "Hey," she cried. "I just realized something—I *have* been doing research for my English paper!"

"Oh, really?" D.J. asked. "Since when did chasing a dog down a runway count as research?"

"Since I realized I could write about the contest, too! It's a great journalistic story—about just how hard it is to be natural," Stephanie said.

"You aren't supposed to work at being natural," D.J. joked. "That's the whole point."

"Exactly," Stephanie said. "Only I wasn't being natural because I wasn't being who I really was. I was trying too hard to be someone else."

"When we all want you to be just Stephanie," Becky said.

"Right," Danny said. "That's your job. Just like it's Michelle's job to be Michelle, and Nicky and Alex's job to be the twins."

"And Comet's job to be our dog," Michelle added.

"This story will be great," Stephanie continued. "I bet no one else in the entire world has ever lost a modeling contest to their own dog before."

"Does that mean you're back to being a writer, Stephanie?" Danny asked.

"No more singing?" Jesse said hopefully.

"No more dress-up?" Becky asked.

"Well, I don't know," Stephanie teased. "I was thinking of giving Club Stephanie another try—"

"Just put it in your story," Joey suggested.

"I guess I will," Stephanie said.

Everyone sighed with relief.

A series of novels based on your favorite character from the hit TV show!

FULL HOUSE™
Stephanie

**Available from Minstrel® Books
Published by Pocket Books**